## "WITTY,
## THOUGHT-PROVOKING . . .
Hayes has created a character reminiscent of Holden
Caulfield in *The Catcher in the Rye*."
*The Schenectady Sunday Gazette*

"A satisfying mystery with an engaging central
character in a tale that bubbles right along—very
good for a first novel with a promised sequel."
VOYA

"Believable and appealing . . . Self-acceptance, the
vagaries of human nature, finding one's niche in the
world—all wrapped in a blanket of mystery involving
a body in a local quarry—make up the elements of
this fine novel by a promising new author."
*The Horn Book*

# THE
# TROUBLE
# WITH
# LEMONS

*Daniel Hayes*

FAWCETT JUNIPER • NEW YORK

RLI: $\dfrac{\text{VL 6 \& up}}{\text{IL 6 \& up}}$

A Fawcett Juniper Book
Published by Ballantine Books
Copyright © 1991 by Daniel Hayes

Library of Congress Catalog Card Number: 89-46192

ISBN 0-449-70416-5

This edition published by arrangement with David R. Godine, Publisher, Inc.

Manufactured in the United States of America

First Ballantine Books Edition: August 1992

20 19 18 17 16 15 14 13

# I

LYMIE TOLD ME we'd be sorry if we went. Which I didn't listen to, seeing how Lymie was the kind of kid who thought you'd be sorry if you got out of bed in the morning. Besides, nobody ever really listened to Lymie. Not even Lymie.

But this time he was right.

I suppose it had to happen sooner or later, Lymie's being right, that is. It's the law of averages or something. And it didn't surprise me that in Lymie's muddled-up mind, his warning me proved that all the trouble that followed was *my* fault. Of course he doesn't say how it was his idea to go swimming, not mine, and if we'd stayed out of the water, nothing would have happened. At least not to us.

Sure, it was my idea for us to sneak out to the quarry that night. But only to see it. Period. I'd discovered the quarry by accident a few weeks earlier and it was wicked cool, this huge basin of gray-green water sitting right there in the middle of nowhere, surrounded by these solid rock walls like a miniature Grand Canyon or something. I couldn't believe my eyes. It was the kind of place part of you'd like to keep all to yourself, but another part of you'd like to bring all your friends to. Only since we were hardly a week into the new school year, and since school was already out for the summer when I moved to Wakefield, and since I'm kind of quiet anyway, all my friends stood for Lymie. And if it wasn't for Mom, I wouldn't've even had Lymie. She'd met Lymie's mother at the Wakefield library one day and after that we used to drive out to this farm she lived on for fresh eggs and milk and stuff. And this lady just happened to have a kid my age, and Mom just happened to invite him over all the time. I knew it was a setup because Mom is one of these lowfat, low-cholesterol people who wouldn't be caught dead eating an egg, and any milk my family used was bound to be skim.

It worked though. Lymie and I did end up being best friends. But not right off the bat. And it wasn't easy. For starters, Lymie and I are like total opposites. I'm a city kid; Lymie's a farm kid. I'm on the thin side; Lymie's on the chubby side. I'm a strict vegetarian; Lymie thinks real men eat cows and pigs and stuff. That kind of thing. But the real problem was Lymie'd always do a million things that'd drive me crazy. Like if he'd see a Porsche or something, he'd make barfing noises and go, "Piece of foreign junk," even though he knew my brother had a Porsche. And if he saw a Trans Am or something jacked up in the back so high it looked like it was getting ready to do a headstand, he'd whack me in the arm and go, "You wanna see a car? Now there's a car." Early on, about the only thing we agreed on was that at least a couple of times a day we'd have to try to punch each other's faces in.

Still for some reason our mothers seemed to think we'd be good for each other.

I asked Chuckie about the quarry (Chuckie's our groundskeeper), and all he told me was to stay away from the place or I'd probably end up drowning because the water was about fifty feet deep all across it. And if I didn't drown, he told me I'd get arrested for trespassing. Big help. Lymie was no better. He'd never even seen it. That really blew me away, him having lived in Wakefield his whole life. Talk about not taking an interest in your environment.

The quarry wasn't much more than a mile from my house and I'd walked there alone quite a few times. They had signs stuck up all over the place warning you to keep out unless you wanted to get prosecuted, and every once in a while somebody did. A couple of nights after I found the place, the Miller sisters were arrested there with two college guys. They were all in the water swimming away and when the cops pulled in with their spotlight and told them to get out, they did. Only according to the two deputies, they weren't wearing anything and the girls started doing like a hula dance or something right on the rocks. In the spotlight. Everybody was talking about it. Their father was some big minister who'd run for the school board because he said there were dirty books in the school library (Lymie checked and couldn't find any), and everybody said he almost busted a blood vessel. He even tried to get the cops fired for not turning off their light.

That story didn't mean much to me, not really knowing these people, except it got me thinking about checking out the quarry at night. Places are different at night, and a place that beautiful in the daytime would probably

3

knock your socks off in the moonlight. But having been raised under streetlights, I'm no Daniel Boone, and traipsing through the wilderness at night wasn't something I was about to do. Not alone anyway.

That's where Lymie figured in. Even though he moans and complains, it's usually not so tough for me to get him to do what I want. I knew Lymie was staying over that Saturday night so I slept in that morning like I do on New Year's Eve or any other day when I know I'll want to stay up late. And as soon as Lymie got there I started building up the place, painting this cool picture in his mind. Plus, I reminded him about the Miller sisters' episode. With Lymie's mentality, something like that elevated the place to a historical landmark practically. It didn't hurt either, my telling him that our housekeeper, Mrs. Saunders, was a heavy sleeper. She wasn't really. But she was kind of heavy. And she would be sleeping.

"It's almost midnight," Lymie had said for about the hundredth time after we left my house. "I must be crazy."

"Yeah, what else is new?" I said finally, backpedaling and watching Lymie chug along, his pudgy face all scrunched up with effort. Between complaints he'd click his tongue and burp. Lymie was always snorting or belching or something, like he thought the whole purpose of his head was to make goofy noises. He's kind of a funny kid.

Passing the last streetlight on the edge of town, we took a left into the shadows and hopped a gate into this huge pasture. With the moon almost full, seeing was no problem. I followed a zigzaggy cow trail, watching my step closely to make sure I didn't step in anything some cow might have left behind. I could hear Lymie muttering and snorting and clicking right at my heels. Pretty soon I slipped through a barbed wire fence on the other side. Nothing but a bunch of brush and some bushes separated us from the quarry now.

"Okay, Lymie, you gotta be quiet till we make sure nobody's there."

"Yeah, Tyler," Lymie sputtered as I tried to unsnag his shirt from the barbed wire, "like the whole stupid world is probably climbing out of bed in the middle of the night and ripping its clothes to get to this stupid place. Duh!"

Lymie always said "duh" when he thought I was saying something dumb. He said it quite a bit.

I started down the narrow path, probably an animal path or something, that led to the water's edge. The brush was alive with mysterious squeaks and twitterings and buzzes. I stood still for a second and pricked up my ears. I could make out the sound of crickets and a few tree toads maybe, but that was it. The rest was pure mystery, like we were surrounded by some kind of strange and secret world out there in the shadows. I felt kind of like Alice in Wonderland or something (if she'd been a guy).

"Lymie," I whispered. "Listen."

Lymie let out this big belch. Then I could hear him scratching himself.

"Listen to what?"

I remembered who I was talking to.

"Forget it," I told him.

"Forget what?" he said. "First you get all spastic and act like you heard something and then you say forget it."

"Just shut up, Lymie."

"You're the one that started talking, dirtbag."

That's the kind of exchange that might have led to us punching each other out earlier in the summer, but we hardly ever did that any more. Lymie didn't notice the same things I did. That's all there was to it. And it wouldn't matter if I beat him over the head with a two-by-four.

We tiptoed forward and before we knew it the path opened into a clearing, and we could see the water. A slight breeze blew our way, and you could tell by the sound of the leaves around us that they were getting ready to change color. They were drier and rustlier than a month ago. And the moon made one of those rippling orange ribbons that stretched from one side of the water to the other. I held my breath. It was beautiful.

I turned to check if Lymie appreciated any of this and was surprised to see he was all wide-eyed. In fact, you'd think he'd just inhaled a fly or something. I looked where he was looking. Across the water on the entrance lane, less than a hundred yards from where we stood, was the lighted red interior of a car. The light hadn't been there a few seconds ago. A guy in a dark jacket climbed into the driver's seat. Another figure sat on the passenger side. Before I could make out much else, the door slammed, plunging the car into darkness again. The engine rumbled, a big V-8 from the sound of it, and the car peeled out, splattering pebbles across the water. Tires screeched as the car skidded onto the highway. Finally the headlights came on, flashing like a strobe light through the trees as the car sped toward town.

"I wonder who that was," Lymie whispered.

"Beats me," I said. "It's kinda weird how they took off like that. Maybe they saw us. You think?"

"Yeah, Tyler, real smart. Like they're old enough to drive and they're gonna panic when they see a couple of eighth graders sneaking through the bushes. Duh!"

"They don't know we're eighth graders, cow breath."

"Oh, yeah, Ty. I forgot how big and tough you look in the dark. We're lucky they didn't have heart attacks right on the spot. We coulda got sued."

He laughed and shoved me to the side in case I might have forgotten he was stronger than me, something Lymie always had to prove. I jabbed at him but without much interest. Big deal, so he thought I was scrawny. I was a runner like my brother Christopher, and no runner in his right mind wanted to be built like Lymie. He might not be what you'd call fat, but he was a little too close to it for my taste.

I sat on the rock ledge dangling my feet over the water. Lymie did too. We were quiet for a long time, looking around and listening to make sure we had the place to ourselves. Gradually I relaxed enough so I could start soaking up the atmosphere. Lymie fidgeted.

"Hey, Lymie," I said, feeling like I had to entertain him, "I'll show you where I scratched my name on the rock wall. It's right under us."

"Boy, Ty, you really know how to show somebody a good time."

We rolled to our stomachs and peered down the side of the rock wall over the water. Lymie struck a match and immediately let out a whoop. Etched in big upside-down letters I saw:

and under that, or over it, I guess, in big scribbly letters:

SUCKS

"Oh, no," I moaned. I swear to God you could carve your name on the inside of a double-locked cast iron safe and when you opened it back up somebody'd've written something nasty about you.

"Whoever did that must know you," Lymie said, elbowing me and yucking it up for all he was worth. " 'Cause they sure got the facts right!"

"Don't be a jerk, Lyme," I told him.

"Hey, *I'm* not the jerk," he said laughing. "You're the one who got caught taking a snooze in Old Lady Waverly's class the other day, not me. My whole bus was talking about it."

I groaned, remembering for the thousandth time how it felt waking up eye to eye with Old Lady Waverly, and everyone in the class giggling and gawking at me. It was like waking into a bad dream. My first week at a new school and already I looked like a total spazola. Exactly the kind of thing Lymie would find amusing.

"You're pitiful, Lymie. You can't appreciate anything unless it's totally stupid."

"Why do you think I hang around with you?" That cracked him up all over again. "Boy, everybody said Old Lady Waverly really went hyper. It must have been great."

"Yeah, Lyme. I'm real sorry you had to miss it," I said sullenly.

Finding a rock, I began scratching out somebody's lame excuse for a joke. Lymie lit matches for me and kept up with the stupid cracks. I scratched out a large area surrounding my name so it'd be harder for anyone else to add their two cents' worth.

"So, Ty, when is Chris coming here again?" The last match flickered out and Lymie rolled to his back and stared up at the stars.

"I don't know." I chucked my rock into the bushes, hard, and turned to my side. "Not till Thanksgiving probably."

"And your mom?"

"In a few weeks maybe. Depends how her shooting schedule goes."

"Awesome," Lymie said. "I can't believe I actually know two movie stars. Me . . . Lymie Lawrence." He grabbed his head. "Then again, why not me? I'm good looking. I'm bright. I'm . . ."

"You're an idiot."

"I'd like a second opinion."

I knew he was waiting for me to say he was ugly too, but I wasn't in the mood to play along. Sometimes I wished my mother and brother did something normal for a living like delivering mail or teaching school. Something where you didn't have to constantly trek all over the planet. It was the same with my father when he was alive. Only he was a producer.

I hadn't seen my mom or Chris since last month when I was in the hospital with a concussion. I'd been sleep-walking and fell down the stairs. (The doctors said that was a first.) Christopher came all the way from our old

9

house in Los Angeles and Mom came all the way from where she was shooting on location in Colombia. First thing Chris said when he saw me was, ''I told Mom we should make you sleep on a leash, Timmy Tyler, but she said your head was unbreakable.'' Mom had poked him in the side and said, ''Now don't you pay any attention to him, Tyler,'' but she knew I didn't mind the teasing.

I answer to a lot of different names. See, Mom wanted to name me Tyler after her favorite uncle, and Dad had insisted on Timothy because he didn't like the name Tyler. Or Mom's favorite uncle either. So I ended up with both names. Mom and Mrs. Saunders called me Tyler (when they weren't calling me ''lamb'' and ''doll'' and that kind of thing), and my dad called me Timothy, and Chris, being in the middle, called me Timmy Tyler. Dad and Mom had already separated before I started school, and Mom put me down as T. Tyler McAllister on all my school records. So that's what I am officially.

''Hey, Ty,'' Lymie said, climbing to his feet. ''Cut the moping act and let's go swimming.''

I sat up and thought for a second. It wasn't really warm enough, but seeing how I'd dragged Lymie there, I said okay. We were both decent swimmers.

Lymie hopped out of his clothes and took a running leap into the water three feet below. Bobbing to the surface, he yelled, ''This is great!'' but knowing Lymie he would've said that if his head had smacked into an iceberg. I was freezing before I was half undressed, so I whipped off the rest of my clothes and dove in before I had a chance to change my mind.

The shock of the cold water took my breath away and

made me a little spastic for a few seconds. I knew pretty soon my teeth would start chattering like crazy. That's something that happens to skinny kids. Lymie could be packed in ice for two days and not get cold.

I warned Lymie not to swim too far from the low rocks about twenty feet to the right of where we'd dove in. That was one of the few places you could climb out without a long struggle. After all, we were naked. What if girls or cops or somebody pulled up in a car? I didn't feel like putting on a show like the Miller sisters.

As usual Lymie ignored me, but I paddled toward the low rocks. When I was close enough for a quick getaway, I rolled onto my back and floated. Kind of. If I didn't kick or stroke every so often, I'd sink like a rock. That's another advantage Lymie had. He could float on his back for a week without so much as wiggling his ears.

I was really getting into the silky cool feel water has when you skinny-dip, staring at the moon, letting my mind drift. Suddenly I felt something sliding down my back.

"Watch it, Lymie, you weirdo."

"What's your problem now, hyper-spaz?"

A shiver shot up my spine which seemed to lift my hair. Lymie's voice was in front of me and quite a ways off. I lay frozen for a few seconds, afraid to move, praying that some big friendly fish was getting into rubbing my backside. Then, taking a deep breath, I flipped to my stomach. My hands pushed into a heavy, wet, woolly thing. As I instinctively thrust the thing away, something rose up out of the darkness into the moonlight. And I saw it.

A face, pale and bloated. And hands, slimy hands reaching for my throat.

I jabbed at it. I kicked at it. I felt the bone on bone of my elbow on its head. As I broke away something slid down my stomach and I came up hard with my knee, so hard my head went under. My feet pushed off it and I came up screaming.

"Lymie! Lymie! OH MY GOD, LYMIE!"

I might have screamed out of control for a week if I hadn't sucked up a mouthful of water. Gagging, I beat a hysterical path toward the shore until my head bashed into the rock ledge. I clawed my way over the bluff, scraping elbows and knees, and flopped belly down on the cold rock platform, choking, gasping for air. Cold water pumped painfully out my nose, and I thought I'd suffocate for sure. My head throbbed and my heart pounded against my rib cage.

Something touched my shoulder and I almost left my body.

"Tyler, you all right? Come on, can you breathe, man?" Lymie was out of breath and his voice trembled.

"Did you see . . ." I gasped, my chest heaving in fits and starts. "Did you . . ."

"Shut up!" Lymie yelled. "I saw it. Just breathe, will you!" He yanked me up and shook me like a rag doll. He probably thought I was having one of my asthma attacks.

"I almost drowned . . . It was grabbing at me!"

"Shut up, Tyler. Just breathe!" Lymie sounded like he wanted to cry, but by now I was crying enough for both of us. He tugged my arm. "Come on. We gotta get dressed and get out of here."

My teeth jackhammered away as I struggled into my

clothes. I kept peeking back at the water, half expecting something to crawl out. I felt my shirt rip as I tried to jam my wet arms through the arm holes. Lymie finished getting dressed and leaned over the ledge.

"I can see it, Ty. Under the water. Come 'ere."

Dropping my other sneaker, I crept up beside him. As much as I dreaded it, I knew I had to look. Maybe I had to see for myself that the thing was dead and powerless. I gasped when I saw it, a man, floating at an incline with arms and legs outstretched, like a freeze frame of a hopping frog.

Then I threw up, right into the water. Lymie held my belt so I wouldn't fall in. He didn't need to worry. There was no way I was going back in there.

# II

E VEN MY ROOM felt cold. I was freezing to death in the comfort of my own home.

We knew we had to call somebody about the body, but we weren't sure who. Lymie said the rescue squad, but I told him that guy was way beyond being rescued. And Lymie said to forget about the village police because the quarry was out of their jurisdiction, and they wouldn't care. So it was a toss-up between the sheriff and the troopers. Lymie knew the sheriff's son and had even been to his house a few times. According to him, the sheriff was a pretty decent guy.

Neither of us wanted to make the call. Lymie claimed the sheriff might recognize his voice, so I was elected. I was still shivering something wicked even though I had thrown on dry pants and two sweatshirts, and I was wrapped in this electric blanket my father's aunt had given me because she said New York'd be cold. I had it cranked up all the way. My breathing still hadn't settled down to the point where talking was that easy. Lymie and I sat on my bed for a while staring at the phone.

"Lymie, I can't. I don't know what to say."

"It's easy, Tyler. Tell them there's a dead guy floating in the quarry. And that somebody should get him out."

"If it's so easy, why don't you do it?"

"I told you. If the sheriff recognizes my voice, I'm dead. My parents would ground me till I'm ready to retire." Lymie picked up the receiver and started dialing. "The longer you wait, the harder it'll be. And remember, NO NAMES." He stuck the phone in my face.

Taking a couple of deep, hitching breaths, I grabbed the phone, closed my eyes, and tried to rehearse what I'd say.

"Sheriff's office." The deep voice sounded tired and annoyed.

"Hello, Sheriff . . . this is . . . ooof!" Lymie had slammed his elbow into my ribs. "Is this who you'd call if you find a person who's dead?" My voice was really shaking now and I had a pretty good idea how stupid I sounded.

"Look, kid, if this is some kind of a joke . . ."

"No, you gotta believe me. This is for real!" I was almost shouting now. "We found this dead guy and we don't know who he is or anything . . ."

"All right. All right. Slow down, son. Take it easy. Where did you find him?" The guy sounded nicer now. He talked slower and softer, like he thought I might be hysterical. I almost was.

"At the quarry. We were swimming." I drew in more air. "I swam right into him."

"I see. And this would be the Wakefield Quarry?"

"Yeah, right outside of town. You better . . ."

"And where are you now? Are you all right?"

15

"Me? Yeah, I'm all right now. But I coulda drowned! I was . . ."

"Settle down, son. Take it easy. How many of you were there?"

"Two of us. My friend and me. Plus the dead guy."

"Listen, son, we're going to need your name and the name of your friend."

"No."

"It's important, son. We need to make sure you're all right. And we'd like to talk to you. I know how you feel. You're afraid that . . ."

Lymie snatched the receiver from my hand and slammed it down. Good thing too, because I can never hang up on anybody, let alone a sheriff.

"Tyler, don't you know they're probably tracing your call? You told them about the body. It's their problem now." Lymie looked at me sitting on the bed all scrunched up in my blanket. "You think they believed you?"

"Yeah, I sounded like too much of a jerk to be playing a joke."

"Boy, finding that body really spazzed you out, didn't it? Your hands are shaking like crazy."

I looked at him. "I don't get it, Lymie. Usually when I wrestle with a dead guy and almost drown, I'm much better than this."

"Sorry. But I've never seen you this way." He paused. "Still pretty cold, huh?"

"I think I'm going to be cold for the rest of my life." I scrunched even tighter into the blanket so only my eyes were showing.

We sat silently. We were both exhausted but neither

16

of us wanted to go to bed. Lymie was clicking his tongue the way he always does when he thinks.

"Ty?"

"Yeah?"

"Who do you suppose he was? I mean, I know you probably don't like to think about it that much, but was there anything about him you can remember? Like how old was he? What color hair? Something."

The bloated face flashed before me again and I felt the cold, slimy hands sliding down me for the fiftieth time. I gulped and fought back another wave of panic and nausea.

"I don't know. It was pretty dark. And I didn't exactly stick around to pose with the guy. He was pretty big, I think. Definitely not a kid."

"Yeah, well, it doesn't matter," Lymie said, putting his feet up and lying back on the pillow. "The police will figure out who he is."

We were quiet for a long time, me huddled up in a ball and Lymie stretched out across the bed.

"Lymie?"

"Yeah?"

"What do you think happened to him?"

"That's easy. He drowned." Lymie sounded half asleep.

"Yeah, but if he was an adult, why would he be swimming at the quarry? That's more like something kids do."

"Who knows. Like he could have been a bum or something, just passing through. And he decided to take a bath, maybe."

"With all his clothes on?"

"Well, maybe he was a bum who was drinking, and he fell in. How should I know?"

"Lymie, what if he was murdered?" The thought sent another chill up my spine. "And what if we saw the murderers?"

"Naw, nobody ever gets murdered in Wakefield. That's city stuff."

"But remember how that car squealed outta there with no lights? I should have told the cops about the car. It might be a lead."

"A lead?" Lymie sat up and rolled his eyes. "You don't even know there was a crime, and already you're finding leads. 'Oh, and by the way, Sheriff, if you happen to see two people drive by in a car, you'd better arrest them. I have reason to believe they murdered someone and tossed them into the quarry.' Duh!"

"Don't be a jerk, hemorrhoid. I'm not in the mood. Besides we know the car had a red interior. And it sounded like one of those big jobbers with a V-8."

"I don't know, Ty. It's almost morning and I'm pooped. Let's go to bed and not think about it any more. By tomorrow they'll have the whole thing figured out."

Lymie stripped down to his underwear and climbed under the covers. Ordinarily when Christopher wasn't home, Lymie slept in his room. He got a charge out of having a room all to himself since he has to share his room with two little brothers. I was relieved he decided to stay in my room without me having to ask. If I was going to have bad dreams and go on another sleepwalking binge, tonight would be the night.

18

# III

T HE FACE RIPPLING in the water was my own. I glided effortlessly across the shimmering surface and the face floated under me, playfully bending and twisting itself into funny house-of-mirrors shapes. I lifted my head, and the face stretched long and thin like a horse's. I touched my nose to the water and the face mashed itself out, wide as a pancake. It was so funny I raised and lowered and turned my head again and again, fascinated by the fish-eye lens distortions of my features. I touched my nose to the water once more but now my nose touched a nose and I could feel it. I heard a "whoosh" and felt a splash as my other face disappeared, like it had been sucked beneath the black waters. I stopped gliding and waited, puzzled at this new game of hide-and-seek. I felt lonely now and wanted to go home. Suddenly a new face appeared, an evil face, pale, bloated, and leering. My heart pounded and I paddled with all my strength, but a strong current held me fast. As I flailed at the water, the face smiled. Rising up from the deep was a pale, puffy body with hands outstretched as if in silent prayer. Icy fingers clutched at my sides, and I screamed louder than I've ever screamed, but no sound came out. I kicked hard into the squishy belly and it burst, a black cloud rising from its tattered white edges. The swollen eyes stared in disbelief as I struck out wildly in every direction.

Now I was dry and running down a long hallway. Boys in blue uniforms with black stripes grabbed at me. I recognized one kid, a fat kid with a high pitched whiny voice. He took my arm and led me to a room, my room. When I turned to thank him, I saw that his face had become the evil face, and I lunged past him, knocking him to the floor. His cold hands snatched at my ankles and tore at my striped pants as I raced out the door, running until my throat and chest burned. The boys lining the hallway watched as I flew by. A foot tripped me, and I sprawled hard on my hands and elbows. Flopping to my back, I saw the boys gaping down at me. They too were wearing evil faces.

A man spoke softly. I knew the voice and peeked up to see my father smiling down at me. His gentle hands lifted me to my feet. My raw elbows throbbed with pain. I tried to tell him what I'd been through, but he didn't understand. When he saw my ripped clothes, he became angry and shook me. I told him it wasn't my fault, but he squeezed harder and shook harder until I squirmed and gasped for air. I grabbed at his hands and felt nothing but bone. Then before my eyes his face melted into a skull. I pulled myself free and suddenly I was alone again, cold and trembling.

Again, a hand on my arm. This time softer, shaking more gently. I pulled away, but I was too tired. I couldn't fight it any more.

"Tyler, honey, wake up. Come on. You're all right now. It's only a dream."

I blinked a few times and squinted up at Mrs. Saunders standing by my bed. Still bleary-eyed, I regarded her suspiciously, making sure I was awake and she was real. Her smile was warm, but her eyes looked worried. I turned to see Lymie wrapped in most of the covers, still snoozing peacefully. My sweatshirts were soaking wet and my pillow felt cold and damp. I grabbed a handful of blankets off Lymie and pulled them around my neck.

"You were having those dreams again, weren't you?" She sat on the edge of my bed and smoothed back the hair that was plastered to my temples. "I thought they had stopped."

"Yeah . . . me too." My voice sounded weak and hollow.

"Is this the first night?" Mrs. Saunders's forehead wrinkled as she peered down at me over her glasses. She was a big woman, and old, but the sort of old that made her seem kind and warm and understanding.

I nodded my head and pulled the covers more tightly around my chin.

"Was it bad? You don't look too good. You want to tell me about it?"

I couldn't keep her questions straight, so I just lay there staring up. She felt my forehead. Her hand was warm and soft and dry.

"You don't feel hot." She stood up, placed her hands on her large hips, and studied me. "Is it possible that the two of you disobeyed orders and decided to stay up half the night watching that trash on 'Chiller Theater'? Now look me in the eye and tell me the truth." She still looked a little worried, but her face was gradually growing more menacing. "Come on. Tell me the truth."

"Uh, uh," I mumbled. "We didn't. We didn't even have the TV on." I could feel her gaze trying to probe my head for secrets. I was too woozy to answer any more questions, so I flipped over and dunked my face into my soggy pillow.

"Well," she said, "I've never known you to lie. But I sometimes suspect you don't always tell me everything you know." Her voice was moving away from me. "But old ladies aren't supposed to know everything boys are up to. I lived through it with your brother, and God willing, I'll live through it with you."

I could hear the shades roll up, and when I lifted my head, the morning brightness splashed over my pillow. I rolled over and sat up, and tried to rub some life back into my head. Mrs. Saunders paused at the door and studied me again.

"If you're planning on running today, honey, you best get a move on. Your brother will be calling at noon."

I do a short run four or five days a week, but Sunday's my big day. I usually get in five or six miles on Sunday morning, and then when Chris calls, I give him my times. But today I didn't feel up to it.

"I think I'll pass on running today, Mrs. Saunders."

"That's fine with me," she said. "I'm always telling your mother I don't think all that running is good for you. You're too thin as it is. Well, come on then. Drag yourself out of bed. Maybe after a nice shower, you'll have enough energy to roll Lyman out. I'll expect you both down at the table in a half hour."

22

After Mrs. Saunders left, I collapsed on my back and managed somehow to slam my head into my headboard.

"Ow!" I popped back up and felt my head for a lump. I looked at my clock and noticed it was almost 11:00. Seeing how Lymie and I hardly ever slept past 8:00, I was lucky I hadn't had to field more questions.

I had to almost cook myself for ten minutes under the steamy water before I was warm clear through. Then I grabbed the soap. Mom told me when I was a little kid that if you used enough soap, you could practically scrub all your troubles and worries away. I knew now that she probably told me that so I wouldn't be so grubby, the way little kids usually are, but it's funny the way a suggestion can stick with you for life. To this day you can always tell my state of mind by how sudsed up I get in the shower. Today, within a few minutes my whole body was lathered up like that guy's face in the Gillette Foamy commercial.

Then I grabbed my lemon shampoo, the same kind I've used since before I could remember. When I was a little kid Christopher used to always call me the Lemon because my hair was so yellow and it always smelled lemony from that shampoo. I used to think that was funny. But then Mom got this car that was always conking out in the middle of nowhere, making her late for work and appointments and stuff. It was in the shop as much as it was on the street. At first I didn't know why, but I'd always stick up for that car, and every time we'd pick it up from the shop I'd tell Mom it was probably all fixed now. And I didn't know why I felt so lousy when Mom got rid of it. Mom couldn't figure it out either. She sat me down and tried to explain how the car had been nothing but a lemon from day one.

23

She told me how she could never really depend on it because even when they'd fix one thing, something else would go. She was always worried because she never knew what it'd do next. And that, she said, was the trouble with lemons. Then it finally dawned on me. Right while I was sitting there. I was just like that car. By the time I was ten, I'd been in and out of more doctors' offices than I could count. Mom and Chris thought it was dopey, me comparing myself to some dumb car, but I couldn't help it. If you looked at things objectively, I'd been ten times as much trouble as that car. And it was probably twenty times more expensive to keep me going. Only you're not allowed to trade in a kid on a new one. Thank God.

I blasted my head with icy cold water and watched the suds swirl down the drain, trying to imagine that each sud was dragging a little trouble down with it. It didn't work. All I could think of was that body.

Throwing on a bathrobe, I went out to check on Lymie. He was still snoozing away like nothing had ever happened.

"Hey, Lymie. Get up. Come on, it's after 11:00." I grabbed his arm and started shaking him. Then I bounced up and down on the bed. One thing you'll never catch me doing is tickling feet. Mom does that and I hate it.

Lymie sat up and looked at me like I was a green alien or something. Talk about a vacant expression.

"Lymie, you awake?" I happen to know people can move around and still not be awake.

"What's your problem, Tyler?" He rubbed his head, grunted, stretched a few times, and then gave me that green alien look again. "Why don't you finish me off?"

"What are you talking about?" I figured maybe he'd been dreaming too.

"Tyler, you scumbag, they oughta make you sleep alone in a padded room." He was definitely awake. "For crying out loud, I should have worn a hockey goalie's uniform to bed. All night long you were rolling around growling and kicking me and jabbing me with your bony elbows. What are you training for—the Olympics or something?"

"Sorry, Lyme." I still felt lousy, but I had to laugh, seeing Lymie scowling at me and looking so crabby. "But it's not my fault you're so delicate. I hope I didn't hurt you too bad."

Lymie muttered something that had the word "kill" in it and stumbled toward the bathroom. I threw on a pair of jeans and a tee shirt. Sitting on the stool in front of the mirror, I began working a comb through my hair. I still looked kind of pale and I felt about the same way. I thought I had finally outgrown these nightmares, but last night they were back as bad as ever.

Only different this time.

When I was little, I had this recurring dream where for some stupid reason I'd always fall off the edge of the earth. I'd hear my mother scream as I fell over this cliff which I never seemed to know was there. I'd fall for the longest time, but when I landed I never got hurt. And I'd look up and see Mom and Dad and Christopher and Mrs. Saunders leaning over looking down at me from the edge of our yard or someplace. They'd always look so sad. I'd yell to them but you could tell they couldn't hear me. Or even see me. It was like I was gone, disappeared, kaput. Mom and Chris and Mrs. Saunders would start to cry, and Dad would lead them away. By then I'd be screaming and jumping around like crazy, even though I knew it wouldn't do any good. Then I'd wake up in a cold sweat, too terrified to even move. By this time, everybody in the house would have come running because I'd been screaming out loud.

I had that dream again after Dad's funeral. When it got real bad there for a while, I started staying in Chris's room with him, and that seemed to help. Chris is a light sleeper, and if I'd start in dreaming and making noise and tossing and turning, he'd wake me up, let me know everything was all right, and I'd go back to sleep. After a few nights, the bad dreams pretty much disappeared. We went through the same thing last month when I started dreaming again and added sleepwalking to my repertoire, and Chris straightened me out in no time flat. But he had his own life to live, and you couldn't expect him to hang around forever to see what stunt I was going to pull next. So when things with me were looking fairly normal, he went back to work in Los Angeles. Mom stayed longer and when she was convinced I was all right, she went to finish her film in Colombia.

Since then I'd been fine.

The doctors told Mom that all this dreaming and sleepwalking probably had something to do with my allergies. Unless people have had some experience with them, they wouldn't believe how bad allergies can be. Just ask me. I could be the poster child for allergic reactions. If there's something around and you can touch it, breathe it, or eat it, there's a decent chance I'm allergic to it. My allergic reactions have run anywhere from regular stuff like itchy eyes and runny nose all the way up to asthma attacks which have almost killed me.

And in between I've had bouts of dizziness, or hyperactivity, or migraines. You name it.

But, all in all, with my shots and stuff things had gotten quite a bit better, and to look at me you'd think I was a regular, everyday kid and not some spazola who was allergic to half the planet.

Besides, any kid that swims into a dead body in the middle of the night is entitled to a few nightmares. I only hoped they weren't back to stay.

Having finished combing my hair, I studied my face. Sometimes I think I'm really starting to look a lot like Christopher, and that makes me feel good. My eyes are dark blue like his, although mine maybe have a little more green in them. And we both have light hair, except his is more wheat-colored and mine is more yellow. My face is a little narrower, but still, lots of times I'll look in the mirror and it's like looking at an old picture of Chris.

But not then. Right then I seemed too pale and too delicate to resemble anyone with my brother's carefree confidence. I tried to look tougher, and stronger, and braver, but all I looked like was a jerky kid making faces in the mirror.

The bathroom door opened, and Lymie's reflection appeared behind me wrapped in a towel.

"You staring at yourself in the mirror again?" he said. "I mean, it's not like you had anything to look at."

# IV

I COULDN'T WAIT to get to Buster's and get the scoop on the body. Buster ran this cruddy game room on the east side of town, and if there was any news, we'd hear it there.

Christopher called at noon. It about killed me not to be able to tell him what happened, but I'd promised Lymie, and paranoid as Lymie was, he stood right over me waving his fist in my face. Mrs. Saunders must have clued Chris in about my nightmare because he asked a zillion questions to find out if something was bothering me. He wondered if I felt bad that he and Mom were going to miss my thirteenth birthday next week. Actually I did, but I didn't want Chris to think I'd have nightmares over something dumb like that. I'm not that big a baby.

Then stupid Lymie got on the phone and started in with the questions about Allie St. John, Chris's co-star. You know, does she take off her clothes in the movie, and if she does, does she take them off right in front of everybody on the set. It was really stupid because if she did take them off, about fifty million people would get to see her, and Lymie was all excited thinking about the cameramen and the lighting crew getting to see her. Plus, what did he think, the camera guys were going to shoot the film wearing blindfolds or something? Chris liked Lymie all right, so he probably didn't mind, but I poked at him until he said good-bye. We had things to do.

On the way out the door Lymie grabbed another chicken leg and a roll. Mrs. Saunders always cooked tons of things like fried chicken and hamburgers and stuff when she knew Lymie'd be around, because except for my dad when he was alive, my family hardly ever ate meat. (I never did.) She said it did her heart good to watch Lymie eat.

"You got it made in the shade, Tyler. You got it made in the shade."

I skipped backward watching Lymie munch his way toward me.

"Why?" I said. "You don't get fed at your house?" I knew that wasn't what he meant, but I wasn't going to make it easy for him.

"Real funny, Ty. You know what I mean. You got a brother with lots of bucks who feels guilty about missing your birthday. And a servant. You practically got your own servant. Made in the shade!" He stopped walking and gnawed on the chicken bone. "Play your cards right and I bet you can get anything you want for your birthday. Anything."

"Cut the crap, Lymie. First of all, Chris probably already bought my present. And second, all's he said was he feels bad about missing my birthday, and you're making a big deal out of it."

"It is a big deal." Lymie lumbered up to me. "That's

guilt you're talking about. And you oughta learn to use it. You know, get the most out of it.''

"You're a jerk, Lymie. You know that. A total jerk.'' I pushed him away from me and kept walking. "And Mrs. Saunders isn't a servant.''

"Yeah, well what is she then, scumbucket? She gets paid, doesn't she? She wouldn't take care of you for nothing, would she?''

"She's more like part of the family. Like a grandmother or something. She took care of Chris when he was a kid too. And I bet she would do it for nothing.''

"Well, if she's like your grandmother, why do you have to call her Mrs. Saunders? I mean if you're paying her, she oughta call you Mr. McAllister.''

"Shut up, Lymie.''

No sense wasting any more breath on the subject. He wouldn't get it anyway. See, my mom had this thing about money and respect, you know, how people who had more money lots of times thought they deserved more respect. She'd even point it out to me if I was watching something like ''The Brady Bunch'' on TV. According to her, it was a prime example of social injustice that Alice, the housekeeper, had to call the parents Mr. and Mrs. Brady, while everyone, including all the kids, got to call her by her first name. And Alice was older than both Mr. and Mrs. Brady, not to mention the kids. When I told Mom that Alice seemed happy enough, she told me that was beside the point because the guys who wrote the show could make even a slave seem happy if they wanted to. Plus, she said, most of the writers had maids, and their kids and everybody probably called them by their first names too.

I thought that was pretty silly at the time, but since

30

then I've seen what she meant. Especially at that snobby prep school my father sent me to. All the maids and gardeners and people like that had to call us "sir" or "Mr. McAllister" or whatever, I guess since we were paying so much to go there. But nobody told us what we had to call them or how we had to treat them, and I couldn't believe the way some of the guys acted. Guys would yell at a maid old enough to be their mother or grandmother, "Get outta here, you old goat. Can't you see I'm busy?" And the poor old lady would have to say something like, "Forgive me, sir. I'll check back later." Because she probably really needed the job and was afraid to complain.

It gave me the creeps to think that Mrs. Saunders might have gotten a job with one of those guys' families instead of ours.

I took off and jogged ahead before Lymie could come up with anything else to discuss. When I reached Main Street I waited for him, so I wouldn't have to walk into Buster's alone. Buster's wasn't the safest place in the world for a new kid. Buster's wasn't even that safe for an old kid.

When we got there, I couldn't believe it. The place was deserted. Buster was sitting on a chair in the doorway wearing his change apron and his usual scowl. He probably tipped the scales at over three hundred pounds, but no one ever let on they noticed. At least not to his face. Every pound of Buster was mean. He had a face like a pit bull. A fat one. And he'd watch the kids every second like he was hoping somebody'd scratch a pool table, or get rough with one of his machines, or cause trouble, or do anything else he wasn't in the mood for. When Buster shook his fist and roared something like,

"Hey, you with the goofy face! Outta here!" every kid in the place made sure his sneakers were packed and ready to go. Because Buster looked at all of us like he thought our faces were goofy, and any of us could have accidentally rubbed Buster the wrong way.

Even though Buster made his living off the town's kids, he acted really put out if you needed change for the games, or were crazy enough to order one of his greasy Buster Burgers. He'd growl, "Whaddaya need now, pigeon face?" and then look down at you like he was wondering whether he could get away with squishing you into the floor. And if a fight broke out, Buster wouldn't even break it up. He'd just pick up a kid in each hand and toss them both out the door onto the sidewalk and snarl, "Go ahead and kill each other, but not around my games."

But it was just as well. With the kind of kids that hung around Buster's, they'd have probably torn the place apart years ago if Buster had treated them halfway decent.

We looked at Buster, and Buster glared at us. Even his chewed-up cigar looked angry.

"Whaddaya want?"

"Hey, Buster, where is everybody?" Lymie asked.

"Do I look like the town historian?" Buster answered. He never could give you a simple answer.

"We thought you might know," I said, squeezing closer to Lymie.

"Yeah, what if I do?" He gave us that "Can I get away with squishing you into the floor" look. Lymie and I stood there waiting. Like fools.

"It so happens I do know," Buster continued. "I figure right now every stupid, nosy, rubberneck in town

32

is out at the quarry watching 'em fish for some bonehead who decided to take his last swim." He chuckled. "Knowing the cops around here, they probably won't find nothing till they drain the place and bring in bloodhounds."

Buster stood up, and Lymie and I backed up.

"Get lost. I'm closing."

"Are you going to the quarry?" I asked. I heard Lymie swallow. Buster looked down at me like I was a mosquito pumping blood out of his arm. I swallowed.

"What's it to ya?"

"Can we ride out with you?"

I couldn't believe my own ears. Here I was having nightmares because of this body, and all of a sudden I get this big urge to go back to where it is. But I couldn't help it. I had to see this thing through to the end. And I didn't even want to waste time walking.

Buster yanked his angry, chewed-up cigar out of his angry yellow teeth and studied me.

"Five bucks. One way. And you keep your traps shut."

I heard Lymie groan.

"Okay, good," I told him. "Deal." I stuck out my hand and really thought Buster might spit on it. I yanked it back.

"That's apiece, baby face. Up front."

I had seven bucks and Lymie only had two. He groaned again but he gave it to me.

"We'll have to owe you one," I said.

Buster snatched the money from my hand.

"I'll trust ya. I never knew anybody that owed me money more than a week."

Buster smiled. Lymie and I didn't.

33

# V

BUSTER OWNED A faded old gray Cadillac with fins pointing out the back that looked like rocket engines. It even sounded like a rocket when Buster tromped on the gas and roared onto Main Street. The guy drove like a total maniac. Sitting between Buster and Lymie, I sank into a few layers of Buster each time we screeched into a hard right turn and got elbowed by Lymie on the lefts. Buster blew thick clouds of cigar smoke that quickly filled up the car. I wondered how he'd take it if I threw up all over his front seat, and I tried to get the thought out of my mind. Thinking about throwing up isn't that far away from actually throwing up.

Dozens of cars lined the road on both sides of the quarry entrance. The people strolling down the lane looked like they could have been going to the county fair. At least until Buster veered in, blasting his horn and swearing out the window. A volunteer fireman in an orange vest planted his feet in front of us and thrust out his arm. Until Buster hit the gas, that is. Then his feet got unplanted pretty quick.

A fire truck, two state trooper cars, a sheriff car, and

a rescue van were parked by the water, all with lights flashing every which-way. A large crowd milled about. The new arrivals craned their necks to see, and the ones who'd been there a while shook their heads and spoke in hushed tones like people do at a wake.

We scrunched up behind Buster as he plowed through the crowd to the water's edge. Way out in the middle a state trooper sat in a blue and yellow trooper rowboat peering over the side into the gray water. Every so often two divers in black suits would surface and direct him to move the boat this way or that. The body must have sunk, and it would probably be tough to spot it in the dark water.

A few yards from where we stood, a large, shapeless woman sobbed quietly and two men tried to comfort her. She kept repeating, "I know it's him. He's never stayed out all night. Oh, God, I know it's him."

The men looked awkward and helpless, and every once in a while they'd say something like, "Now, Claire, we don't even know for sure anyone is in there."

But it didn't do any good. She seemed to know, as surely as Lymie and I knew, that a body *was* in there, and it was pitiful to watch her stunned misery. The men might as well have shut up. There was no way anybody could make her feel any better.

I turned away and fixed my eyes on the water, and closed them pretty fast when I remembered what might come floating up. Suddenly I wanted to get out, to be as far away from the poor woman and the body as possible, but I was walled in by people. I wished I could go do something, play basketball, run, anything that would take my mind off this woman, and the body, and all the misery and suffering that come from tragedies like this one. I drew in a deep breath and tried to stop thinking, but it was too late. My mind was already back to last summer. The worst summer I'd ever had.

Dad had been furious that I'd screwed up so bad at prep school, less than three months there and they didn't even want me back. I told him I wouldn't have gone back anyway, and that sent him through the roof again. My allergies were going crazy, and I was practically a basket case. By early August I'd had three or four asthma attacks within a month, as well as a bunch of other symptoms that came and went, like dizziness, and nosebleeds that wouldn't stop, anxiety, nightmares, you name it. I'd spent half my summer in one doctor's office or another as they all tried to find out what was going wrong. Mom blamed Dad for having insisted I be sent away to military school. And Dad said I had pretty serious problems before I ever even heard of Grant Academy. They fought whenever they saw each other, which was usually only on weekends when Dad stopped by to see me or take me someplace. I was terrified that one time he'd decide not to come back, that I just wasn't worth it.

When things seemed to be about as bad as they could get, Chris woke me one morning saying he needed a vacation, so why didn't we take off for a few days. He had the keys to a friend's cabin on Lake Granby, in Colorado. I couldn't believe it. Chris never took time off in the middle of a picture, and I knew it was me who he figured needed a vacation, but I didn't wait to be asked twice. We left before breakfast, flew to Denver, rented a car, and were floating on the lake by evening. It happened so fast, it didn't even seem real. It was like living in a dream.

36

If it's possible for a person to be happier than I was those three days on the lake, I'd be surprised. Prep school, and doctors, and allergies, and arguments seemed to belong to another world, one I could only vaguely remember. Our cabin was surrounded by a dense, cool forest which crept up to the brightest, bluest lake you could ever imagine, a place right out of a postcard. Every day Chris and I would go out in a boat for hours and fish and swim and talk. The water was so clear sometimes it felt like we were floating on air. In the late afternoon we'd hike up the side of the mountain or around the lakeshore and see deer and rabbits, and birds I didn't even recognize. When evening came, I'd bustle around collecting firewood, and we'd cook outside as the sun disappeared behind the trees. Then we'd sit around the campfire talking for hours. I told Chris all about prep school, and it was like talking about the scary part of a fairy tale, where you knew no matter how bad things got, everything would turn out happily ever after. And I told him how one of these days I'd make Dad proud of me even if he wasn't now. Then I'd fall asleep outside staring up at the stars, bright sparkly ones, not your dingy L.A. kind. I'd wake early in the morning, snug and warm in my sleeping bag, to a world that was kind and clean and where nothing bad could get in.

Each morning we'd drive to this little store and call Mom, and I'd tell her about the place and tell her she was crazy not to fly there right away. Then Chris would send me inside to pick up whatever supplies I thought we'd need for the day. And at eleven years old, I felt smart to know they wanted to talk about me, how did I feel, was I happy, that kind of thing. It was a world created for me, all mine, and five senses weren't enough to take it all in.

I even got thinking that Mom and Dad would get together again. My allergies would disappear, and Dad would never dream of sending me away to a boarding school again. We'd all be one big, happy family. I thought all this and believed it.

Until the fourth morning.

It was Tuesday, a beautiful Tuesday, with the bright morning sun peaking through the trees and a cool breeze blowing across the open porch of the store. This time Mom stopped me when I started in. She told me the news that only I hadn't known. Four days earlier, a private jet carrying Dad to New York had gone down somewhere north of Flagstaff. The searchers combing the area had finally found the wreckage. There were no survivors. Dad, his business manager, and the pilot were all dead. I felt like I'd been slammed hard against the wall, hard enough to knock the wind out of me. But I didn't cry. I couldn't. Something inside me had stopped. And that's the part that would have cried.

I don't remember much of the trip back to Los Angeles. I had been yanked out of my dream world so fast that my mind was reeling with a kind of mental whiplash. Chris talked to me a lot but I didn't know what he said. And I didn't say a word. There was nothing to say.

At the airport Mom took my arm and led me to the car. She spoke softly into my ear, and Mrs. Saunders patted my knee as Chris drove home. A while later we turned onto the Santa Monica Freeway. I remember that I had trouble sounding out the letters on the huge green sign. And even when I did recognize the words, I didn't see any point to them.

Or to anything else.

I coughed once . . . twice . . . and I felt an awful tightness gripping me from behind my ribs. It was like someone huge was sitting on my chest. I sat bolt upright, and listened, as if I were outside myself, to the slow, wheezy breathing. My pulse quickened as every muscle in my chest, my whole body, struggled to draw in air. I felt like a distant observer, watching some stupid kid whose shocked eyes bulged, and whose hands grabbed for air that couldn't be grabbed. Somebody pushed my head forward over my knees, and I heard a voice shout, "He's turning blue!" It sounded like Mom, but it was coming from far away. I heard coughing that became more violent, and I felt pity for this frightened body which didn't even have the sense to breathe.

Bright lights buzzed over me, and strangers in white held my head over my knees. Words floated by me like cartoon captions. I felt I could have grabbed them if I sat up. Certain words came by more than once, and they took on colorful, three-dimensional shapes. "ASTHMA . . . NURSE . . . ADRENALIN." The words didn't mean anything to me. They were just shapes and colors.

I tried to raise my head and couldn't. Something cold was put on my arm. A sharp stabbing pain over the cold spot made me jump. I struggled to get loose, trying to remember where I was and why I was being handled by so many people. I couldn't. A light tremor grew from inside my heart into shaking that I could watch in my arms and legs. I heard crying and was surprised to realize it was my own. I cried harder and harder and someone said it was all right. Even though I was crying much harder than Dad would have ever allowed.

Once I pulled out the stops, that was it. I was crying like crazy and I couldn't stop. I cried until I hardly even knew what I was crying about. And I didn't care if Chris saw me or anyone else. And that was strange for me. Even when I was little I never gave in like that. It was almost like I was crying for all the other times that I'd held it in. And even though I was more miserable that night than I'd ever been, there was something good about letting go. Like an awful weight had been lifted from my chest.

As I listened to this woman sobbing pitifully, I knew how helpless everybody must have felt being with me that night. There was nothing anybody could do for her. It was something she'd have to go through on her own.

Suddenly I was startled by a change in the crowd. It had grown quieter, more attentive. Opening my eyes, I saw one of the divers disappear under the water. The trooper in the boat was hunched over the edge peering down, but more intently than before. The spectators slowly and silently crowded the rocky rim, and I sat down, afraid I'd be squeezed into the water.

"Looks like they got him." Lymie's whisper startled me. I'd nearly forgotten he was next to me.

The divers and the trooper were awkwardly hoisting something from the water. As the boat tipped up, we could see the body of the drowned man. My stomach lurched and I looked away. When I looked back, the boat had straightened up and most of the body was hidden on the bottom. Both divers had scrambled into the boat after it.

The sobbing woman was silent now, not even breathing, with a hand across her heart and leftover tears in her eyes. She started bouncing slightly and wrapped her hands around her jaw like some game show contestant waiting to see if her answer was right for the grand prize. I hoped like crazy she'd be wrong, and the body would be someone who didn't belong to anybody. The woman turned away from the boat, walked a few paces from the water, wrung her head, and returned. She did this two or three times, until the boat reached the edge a few feet below us. The two men around her held her arms as she leaned dangerously over the water. All she needed was a peek, and this awful wail rose from her throat. She would have toppled into that boat for sure if the guys hadn't yanked her back. She screamed and kicked at them as they dragged her away. A few more hands fumbled to help control her, but most of the crowd backed off looking stricken and helpless.

"Tyler, it's BooBoo Anderson!" Lymie's eyes were wide and his jaw had dropped.

Almost against my will, my head turned to watch the body being lifted toward the waiting stretcher. I almost gagged but I kept looking. It was bloated some and kind of pale, but not as bloated or pale as I remembered it. Big, fat Buster, perched on his hands and knees, gently lifted the body onto the stretcher and his face almost looked tender and sad. When the body landed, water gurgled out the mouth past the blue lips and splashed down the chin. My stomach reeled but my eyes kept watching. As the stretcher was lifted, he gurgled some more water up. Finally a rescue squad guy came running up with a white sheet and covered him up.

Buster cleared a path for the men carrying the body, and they headed for the van. The air seemed hollow, and whenever anybody coughed or anything, you could almost hear an echo off the rocky ledges. Staring wide-eyed at the body, I had nearly forgotten about the sobbing woman, but suddenly she broke free of the men and charged the stretcher. She snatched the sheet up and screamed, "Bobby, Mommy's here now! Listen to me, Bobby! Mommy will take care of you."

She shook the body like she thought she could wake it up. She had this distant kind of scary look, as if she were possessed by demons or something. When her son didn't move, she flung herself at the stretcher and nearly toppled him off it. Buster gently but firmly lifted her up, and led her through the crowd past where we could see.

Lymie and I stayed sitting on the edge of the rock wall, neither of us caring to see any more. I was thinking about BooBoo and about how I'd never even heard his real name before or even wondered what it was. I never thought about him as having a mother or anything like that. BooBoo, or Bobby as his mother called him, worked at the school. I'm not sure if he was a janitor or only a janitor's helper, but I'd seen him a lot working around school my first week. He must have been around twenty or so, and I think he was a little retarded. He got his nickname because when he talked, he sounded like BooBoo, Yogi Bear's sidekick. If a water pipe or something would break, he'd say to his boss in this sad, nasally voice, "Gee, Mr. Bremmer, what'll we do now?" That cracked everybody up when he did that. Especially the kids who weren't much smarter than BooBoo to begin with.

But he was a nice guy. On the second day of school, after I'd been thrown out of Old Lady Waverly's class for sleeping while I was supposed to be filling out a stupid worksheet, he saw me sitting on a chair outside Mr. Blumberg's office. I was feeling pretty low. BooBoo pulled up another chair and asked me who I was. When I told him who I was and what I'd done, he really seemed to feel bad. I told him how everybody'd laughed at me, and he said, "That's all right. They laugh at me too. Just don't forget, they've done dumb stuff too."

I even ended up telling him how it was easier for me to fall asleep around a crowd of people, like in a classroom, than it was for me to fall asleep alone in my room at night. And I never told people that kind of stuff. He wanted to know all about California and I told him. He said he wanted to go there someday. Before he left, he told me that Old Lady Waverly used to put him to sleep too, and that didn't mean I was bad.

That really got to me, BooBoo caring enough to worry about whether I thought I was bad.

My stomach sank thinking about him drowning.

Buster growled from behind for us to get into his car, and he'd drop us off in town. When we looked suspicious, he told us there was no charge. We could hardly believe it. And not only that, but he drove us right to my house. As we were climbing out of his car, he mumbled, "That BooBoo. He spent a lot of money at my place."

That's what he said. But I looked at him. And I don't think he cared at all about the money.

# VI

"AW, CRAP!"

I almost barfed all over my assignment pad. I looked again, and I still didn't believe it. Over the weekend I was supposed to have collected twenty rocks for Old Lady Waverly and be able to tell what each one was by looking at it, feeling it, and scratching it on things. What a way to end a perfectly lousy weekend. As if I didn't have enough on my mind.

"What's the matter, dear?" Mrs. Saunders yelled from downstairs.

"Nothing. Just my stupid, idiotic, lamebrained science homework!"

"Well, don't be long. It's getting late."

It was getting late all right. I had finally finished all my other work, and I could barely keep my eyes open. I almost climbed into bed without even being told. Then when I flipped my pad open to double check, I saw the science assignment. I couldn't believe it. And Old Lady Waverly would be in all her glory if I showed up empty-handed.

I stumbled downstairs and out the door in a kind of sleepy version of panic. It was too dark and I didn't have the ambition to search the whole yard, so I ended up grabbing a bunch of rocks from the flower beds. I thought I'd struck the jackpot. I lugged them upstairs in a paper bag and dumped them on the floor.

"Aw, crap!" I stared in disbelief at the bright red, white, and blue stones the old owners had left behind. "Why me?"

"What's the matter now, dear?"

"My stupid, moronic science rocks! They're painted like Fruit Loops."

I found a file and started scraping them down, but it didn't do any good. All of them were the same kind of crushed stone. And there wasn't one listing for crushed stone in the whole stupid science book.

I was trying to decide whether to slit my wrists or go outside for another bunch of rocks when Mrs. Saunders came in and told me I had to go to bed.

"Come on, Tyler. Your work will keep. Right now you need your rest." She smiled when she saw my stupid red, white, and blue rocks and put them back in the bag.

"It's easy for you, Mrs. Saunders. You don't have to face Old Lady Waverly tomorrow with those goofy looking things." Even though I was pouting, I was really glad to get to bed. I told myself I'd get up early and find some more rocks.

I didn't. I should have known. Monday morning is the pits. That's one thing you can always count on. When Mrs. Saunders woke me up, I was so groggy I felt like I'd been drugged. It took all my concentration just to get out of bed and take a shower. I did make it to school on time, barely, and that was only because Chuckie happened to be painting the front porch when

I came stumbling out of the house ten minutes late, dropping my books all over the driveway, and he gave me a ride. I weaved my way through groups of loud, laughing kids who didn't have enough brains to be miserable, and sped up the stairs to my locker.

Mary Grace Madigan was calmly organizing her locker and sorting out all the books she'd need for the morning. Exactly what I needed to see. It's kids like her who make kids like me look worse than we really are. Mary Grace sat behind me in nearly all my classes because her name was after mine on the teachers' alphabetical lists. For some reason the Mc in McAllister is alphabetized under Mac. That's also why her locker was next to mine.

I scooted up beside her and tried three or four different ways of dialing 40-20-8, as half the messy stack of books and papers I'd scooped up from the driveway started slipping out from under my arm and tumbled around my feet. The lock finally released and I pulled the handle up and out. The bottom of the locker door gaped open an inch or so, but the top was jammed. I jiggled the handle up again and yanked harder until the door flew open and banged me in the nose. The remaining books dropped from under my arm, and a few others toppled out of my locker and piled up with the others around my feet. I groaned. Nice way to start a new week! I crouched down and began stuffing layers of junk on top of the other layers of junk already at the bottom of my locker.

"You're funny. You know that?" Mary Grace, having finished making her locker look like something out of *Better Homes and Gardens*, was standing above me looking down at my jumbled mess of books and papers.

"You probably love it when people fall down the stairs, too," I said.

"Depends who it is," she said, laughing. "Look, you want some help? I'm good at this. Really."

She didn't wait for an answer. She brushed past me and began pulling everything from my locker, including the large textbooks and permanently twisted notebooks wedged on the bottom, and began stacking them neatly up on the shelf. Before I knew it, my books were perfectly arranged in a beautifully tapered pile, titles facing out, and the books I needed for the morning were waiting in a neat pile at my feet.

"How could you possibly do that to a locker in less than a week?" She shook her head in disbelief.

"I don't know. It's a gift, I guess."

She laughed. "Do you clean your own room at home? I can't imagine."

"Kind of. Well . . . sort of," I said and then I laughed too. "Not really."

If Mrs. Saunders didn't help me keep my room straightened up, our house might have been condemned by now. I'm the only one in my family who's a total slob. If I didn't look a little like Chris, everybody probably would have thought I was adopted or something. It drove Mom and Dad crazy. It was the one thing about me they agreed on. Dad, being a former military man, couldn't stand any kind of clutter. And Mom said it was deplorable that I thought since I was a boy I didn't have to pick up after myself. I told her that wasn't fair. I know if I'd been a girl, I still would have been a slob. It's just . . . I don't know . . . I always seem to have other stuff on my mind.

One time Mom told Mrs. Saunders not to go near my

room. Mom always warned me about Mrs. Saunders's heart not being so great, and maybe she figured cleaning a room like mine could really hurt her. Plus she probably wanted to see how rotten I'd let it get. After a few days she marched me up there with a vacuum cleaner, a laundry basket, and a Hefty garbage bag, and told me not to set foot outside the door until my room looked the way a room should look. That meant the way she thought a room should look. Christopher tossed in a baseball bat and told me to use it if I saw any suspicious movements under all the crud. And he said not to worry, that he'd sneak food to me every day. Ha, ha. Later that afternoon, Mrs. Saunders came sneaking in and gave me a hand. It was to be "our little secret." She said, "Don't you worry, Tyler. I used to have to tidy up after your father and your brother too, and they didn't even know it. A man just can't clean the way a woman can."

She was careful not to talk like that in front of Mom. Mom was always trying to liberate Mrs. Saunders. When Mom would start in on her "this is the twentieth century" lecture, Mrs. Saunders would always wink at me. I think she knew Mom wouldn't have much luck at reforming either of us.

I looked down at Mary Grace's pile of stuff.

"Hey, Mary Grace. Where's your science rocks?"

"Home. They're not due till next week, remember."

"Oh, yeah, right." Something inside me did a cartwheel.

Mary Grace hurried off to homeroom almost before I could thank her. I watched her for a moment, thinking. Mary Grace was one of the prettiest, most popular girls in the eighth grade. I wondered if she kind of liked me, or if she thought I was some kind of pathetic pig. I couldn't tell.

I slipped through my homeroom door right as the bell went off and joined the other kids in mumbling the "Pledge of Allegiance." Then after a few warm-up clicks and rapping noises, Mr. Blumberg's voice came over the P.A. system with the morning announcements. The first thing he did was ask for a moment of silence in memory of Robert Anderson, who he said would be sorely missed around school and around town. I hadn't even formed a good picture of BooBoo yet when Mr. Blumberg raced on with the rest of the announcements. No crying over spilt milk for that guy.

Everybody was talking about BooBoo all day, but nobody knew that much. At lunch, Jeff Hunter, whose father was county sheriff, told us that some scared little kid had called a deputy in the middle of the night to report finding the body. The cops were hoping that little kid, or the other kid that was with him, would come forward so they could get more information out of them. As it stood they didn't have much to go on. They could tell that BooBoo had suffered a knock on the back of his head, but that could have happened if he fell in. They were hoping the coroner's report would turn up something.

A scared little kid. I was glad Lymie hadn't let me give names. And Lymie was glad we wouldn't get caught.

"Really, Ty, it was good you sounded like such a little jerk. They'll never guess in a million years that the body was found by a couple of eighth graders."

"Thanks, Lyme," I said. "Anything to help."

After seventh period, Mary Grace helped me pack the

49

books I'd need to bring home, figuring in which work I'd be able to get done in study hall the next day. She had eliminated most of the guesswork from school. She knew which teachers graded on neatness and punctuality, which ones admired original thought, and which ones wanted nothing but their own words flung back at them on exams. I couldn't believe it.

"You're in the top group, Tyler, and you need to know these shortcuts. But don't worry. Since you're new here, I can fill you in."

But it didn't matter that I was new. Not really. Schools were always kind of mysterious to me. Most teachers I'd had seemed to like me all right, even though most said I worked below my potential. But success or failure was hit or miss with me, like walking through a mine field and hoping you didn't get blown up. But for kids like Mary Grace, it was like they had studied the mine field and drawn maps so they never accidentally stepped on anything that would go bang. It wouldn't hurt being more like that. And it sure would have made Dad happy.

We walked down the front steps of the school toward the street.

"Wasn't it awful about BooBoo Anderson?" Mary Grace said. "He was the sweetest guy."

Everybody claimed to feel bad about BooBoo but with Mary Grace it was different. She didn't sound excited, like it was some fun kind of mystery or something.

"Yeah," I said. "That was pretty bad."

"I can't help thinking about those poor little kids who found him. Imagine little kids running around on their own in the middle of the night. Some parents, huh?"

50

We had almost reached Main Street. I watched the way the breeze and the sunlight played through her sandy hair.

"Maybe they weren't so little," I said. "That old deputy probably thinks anybody under thirty is a little kid. Plus, they probably sneaked out. And maybe they couldn't tell their names because they had the kind of parents who'd really be upset if they knew their kids were outside fiddling around at night."

"Maybe," she said. "But I bet those kids are having some kind of nightmares after that experience."

I knew one of them was.

I left Mary Grace in front of her house and kept walking home. I almost wished I had told her.

# VII

IN THE FEW months since I'd come to Wakefield, I hadn't gotten to know Chuckie very well. I'd see him every day as he worked around the yard or fixed up the house, which Mom wanted restored to its original condition, but Chuckie didn't talk much. He'd answer me if I asked him a question, barely, and he'd say hi if I said hi, but that was about it. I figured maybe he didn't like kids too much. Or maybe he thought I was some kind of spoiled rich brat.

I did know that Chuckie had just gotten out of the marines or something, and that he held black belts in both judo and karate. I also knew from Lymie that he had quite a reputation around town; nobody messed with Chuckie Deegan. Even though he was six feet tall and real muscular, he moved with the smoothness and grace of a cat. Like he could walk through the woods without crackling the leaves.

I'm not sure what his official job description was, but I figured that in addition to keeping up the place, Mom had asked him to keep an eye on Mrs. Saunders and me. I knew that even with all his references, Mom wouldn't have hired him unless he agreed to live in the guest cottage at the edge of our property. Being in the movies made Mom kind of a public figure. Which she didn't mind so much for herself; she said that went with her career. Besides, she knew how to handle people and crowds and everything. But I was quite a bit quieter, more shy, and even though we moved here because Mom thought small town life would be good for me, I think she worried that outside L.A., where celebrities are a dime a dozen, people might bother me all the time. They didn't. Sometimes I'd see kids gawking at me. And a couple of times some girls came up to me, all giggly and trying to hide behind each other, wanting to know if I was Linda LaMar's son (LaMar is Mom's maiden name), but mostly everybody left me alone. Since Chris's first big movie wouldn't be out till around Christmas, and since my last name is different from my Mom's, maybe a lot of people just didn't make the connection. Who knows?

Anyway, since Mom knew she'd have to be away from time to time, it didn't surprise me that she'd hire some tough guy like Chuckie to be around and keep an eye on things. And I didn't figure there was much more to know about Chuckie. He was the tough, silent type, and that was that. Only on Tuesday, I found out that wasn't that. Because sometimes a person will do something for you, some little kindness or whatever, and it's one of those things you know you'll never forget for the rest of your life, no matter what. And that's how I came to consider Chuckie part of my family, the same as we all considered Mrs. Saunders part of the family.

By Tuesday I still hadn't recovered completely from the whole BooBoo thing, and I was kind of counting on a normal day with no hassles. After school Mrs. Saunders was driving me to Albany for my weekly allergy shot, and then we'd go out to dinner and maybe see a movie or something. I was kind of looking forward to it this week. I needed to get away from Wakefield for a few hours. I'd already made it through three periods, and I was hoping to lay back and coast through the rest of the day, no sweat.

Then disaster struck. Disaster has lots of faces, but this time it appeared in the form of Beaver Bruckman. Beaver was one of those kids who'd probably been in the eighth grade since the school was built. And since the junior high wing was like his permanent home, he probably figured he had seniority rights over the smaller, scrawnier kids who were merely passing through. Half the kids who experienced a growth spurt in last year's eighth grade class thought it was because Beaver had picked them up so many times by the head.

The only class Beaver was good at was gym. In fact, in gym he was the undisputed king. But you had to watch out for him. By fourth period gym class every day, Beaver had stubble on his chin, and the friction of exercising with stubble might have made him irritable or something. In touch football, Beaver's touch was more like a full body slam. Kids were so scared of him, he could block by giving a dirty look. And if you were lucky enough to make it through the game in one piece, you still had to make it through the shower. Beaver was the kind of kid who got his jollies by reaching over and turning your faucet to scalding, and he'd actually get mad if you didn't stay under it and burn. Then came towel snapping. Beaver would always dampen the towels to improve their action, and he could make them crack like a whip. One guess what his favorite target was. Beaver was one guy you *had* to turn your back on. And he was persistent too. Last Friday he snapped at me so much, I felt like I'd been blow dried.

Each day after getting into our gym clothes, we'd dash out to the gym floor for attendance and the word or two of daily instruction which made up the phys. ed. curriculum. Today's lesson, which Mr. Johnson delivered in a voice that must have started down around his ankles was, "Laps," and then he chucked a football at the kid closest to him. I knew from last week that the "laps" part meant we had to go outside and run four laps, and the football meant we'd pick up sides for a touch football game. The first kid to finish would get to be a captain and Mr. Johnson would pick the other captain. So far it'd always been Beaver who finished first. And Mr. Johnson would always pick this other humongous kid, Ralph Martin, to be the other captain.

"Lymie, buddy," I said as we trotted out to the track, "Today I'm gonna get to be a captain."

I took off ahead at an easy pace and smiled when I heard Lymie yelling for me to stop. I'd plodded along with him every other day, but today, for some reason, I really wanted to be captain. I don't know . . . maybe I needed to feel like I had some control over my life. Anyway, I was used to running five miles with Chris, and when Chris was away, I worked on increasing my speed because I knew he always had to run slower than he'd like to so he wouldn't leave me behind. I wanted to be as fast as him by the next time he came home. Not only that, but running was also making my lungs stronger and would probably cut down on the chances of my having another serious asthma attack.

I hadn't run since Saturday morning. I really hadn't

been sleeping all that great since swimming into poor BooBoo's body that night and I was waking up later than usual. And since Mrs. Saunders thought rest was more important than running, she never got me up for school until it was too late for me to go out and run. And I'm a morning runner. By Tuesday I felt fine and light like you do after you've laid off for a few days. Four laps was a piece of cake. It was only a mile. I knew I'd win easy, and I could be captain of my own team.

I wished Christopher could have been there to see me. I finished half a lap ahead of everybody else. Mr. Johnson told me he'd like to see me on the track team next year and that I should keep practicing and stay off the booze and cigarettes. I laughed. I couldn't picture myself sitting around with a six pack of beer and a pack of Winstons.

Mr. Johnson picked some other smaller kid to be the other captain, probably so the teams would be fair. I picked Ralph Martin first so we'd have at least one big guy. Then I picked Lymie. I didn't pick Beaver even though he was probably the best player because I figured he'd try to run the team. Lymie wasn't too thrilled about the whole thing. I heard him mumble, "You'll be sorry." But that's the way Lymie is. How was I supposed to know that Lymie would be right for the second time in less than a week? What are the chances of that happening, like a thousand to one?

The first time I went out for a pass, Beaver was right there covering me, and rather than going for the ball like he was supposed to, he slammed me hard into the ground. I hit so hard I got dirt in my mouth. I called pass interference, but Beaver said he never touched me.

56

I looked over at Mr. Johnson, but he seemed to be daydreaming. Probably thinking about lesson plans for his next class, I thought angrily. Beaver called it an incomplete pass, and nobody argued it.

On the next play, Beaver sideswiped me before the ball was even close, jabbing his elbow into my ribs for all he was worth. I called pass interference again, and Beaver swore again he never touched me. Now I was mad. My whole body tensed up with rage, and I wouldn't have backed down for ten Beavers. I didn't care. I mean what could he do, anyway? Brushing past him, I grabbed the ball and moved it to where he had slammed me. When I straightened up, Beaver's face appeared in front of my face. It was almost deadpan, except for the clenched teeth and the hate in his eyes.

"You callin' me a liar, rich boy?"

"You slammed me," I said, backing up a step. "Let's just play the game, all right?"

"Tell me I'm a liar!" He pushed hard into my chest and I fell back another two steps. My whole body shook with fear and anger.

"Tell me I'm a liar, rich boy. Come on." Another push, harder this time, and I nearly landed on my butt. I stood facing Beaver's cruel eyes.

"Are you chicken, rich boy?" I could smell Beaver's hot, sour breath. "Whaddaya sleepin'? Wake up, boy."

He cuffed me a good one on the side of the head, hard enough to knock me sideways a good couple of feet. Before I knew it, all the anger and fear and pain I'd ever felt burst through my arm with an almost electrical jolt. My fist caught the hard jaw before the mouth had formed its next taunt. I heard teeth grind under my knuckles. I knew I was dead meat now, and knowing that electrified my entire body, my arms windmilling punches, and my legs driving me forward into Beaver. I could feel myself being hit back, but I felt no real pain. It was like my heart was pumping novocaine instead of blood. Then large powerful hands yanked me in a semicircle, and a large body wrapped around me and held me in a tight grip.

"That's enough! Stop it now!" The voice in my ear was Mr. Johnson's, and the arms holding me down were Mr. Johnson's. Now they jerked me to my feet.

"McAllister, go in and get yourself cleaned up. And Bruckman, sit on the bench. Somebody should have hit you years ago."

Beaver's nose was dripping blood which trickled over the corners of his mouth and swollen lips like a bloody Fu Manchu. His eyes smoldered with hatred. He took one last seething look at me before retreating to the bench.

My tee shirt was bloody, but with whose blood I didn't know. I could taste blood around the corners of my own mouth. When I touched my face, it felt wet, and my hand turned magically red. I probably staggered a little because Mr. Johnson grabbed my arm. He tipped my head back, jiggled my nose, and looked into my mouth. Then he patted me on the back and told me again to get cleaned up.

Now that Beaver was out of range, a few kids mumbled, "Good for you, Tyler. He had it coming."

My head pounded something fierce and I felt lousy, but something inside me felt good about not letting myself be pushed around. I spit and a few specks of blood landed on the new white sneakers Mom had bought me for school. I knew this wasn't over. Not by a long shot. Beaver didn't strike me as the forgive and forget type.

Mom always told me I had a temper like Dad's, and she didn't mean that as a compliment. Mom claimed she never hit anybody in her whole life, and I believed her. I could remember the long, loud fights she and Dad would have if he hit me. The worst time was after Dad got the letter saying I wouldn't be allowed back to Grant Academy in the fall because I'd been in too many fights and wasn't adjusting, according to them. Mom had to climb right in between us that time. Dad had me by the neck and was all set to belt me when Mom wedged herself between us and pushed on him so hard it pinned my head against the wall. That was as close as I ever saw my mother to getting hysterical.

She screamed, "Only an idiot would hit a child to teach him to stop fighting!" Then she told him if he ever touched me again, she'd get a court order to prevent him from seeing me.

Dad had shouted, "You're to blame for all his problems, not me! I could straighten him out in a week if you'd let me."

It would have been ten times easier to have gotten belted. I was pretty mad at Mom because now I was sure Dad was gone for good. I was wrong. He picked me up the next Sunday at the usual time. But he never mentioned Grant Academy again. And I never had a chance to explain my side of things. Never.

Chris took after Mom. He had more patience than anyone I knew, and I had never known him to fight. Even when I blew up at him for some stupid reason, he wouldn't get angry. I'd be swinging and kicking like some kind of crazy person, and he'd just move in on me and pin me down. And he'd say something like, "Listen to me, Timmy Tyler, in a second I'm going to let you go. And if you still want to hit me, you can. But I'd rather you tell me what you're really upset about." I couldn't get into hitting him then. And it was funny, after we talked, I usually discovered it wasn't even him I was really mad at.

I wished Chris were around now. I tried to think how he would have handled Beaver, but I couldn't figure it out. Chris wasn't the kind of guy to back down from what he knew was right. But still, I couldn't picture him carrying on like I did. I really didn't know what he'd've done. As I got dressed I wondered if I'd ever reach the age where I wasn't always so confused about things. I doubted it.

The rest of the day I was treated pretty good by everybody. Kids I didn't even know came up and told me they wished they had been the one to smack Beaver around. It felt good to know kids were pointing me out saying, "Yeah, that's the kid that belted Beaver in gym class." My lips were cut inside from where they had been mashed into my teeth, and my nose was feeling a little sensitive, but I felt pretty decent.

Until lunch when I saw Lymie. Mr. Doom and Gloom.

"So how are you planning to get home, Ty?"

"I'm gonna walk, same as usual."

"Yeah, that's real bright, Ty. Like Beaver isn't going to mash your face into the sidewalk as soon as you step outside the school."

"You're always such an optimist, Lyme." I tried to act like his words didn't bother me that much. "Besides, he'd really look stupid beating on me. He's twice my size."

"Duh, real good, Ty. Like Beaver's gonna stop and think like a regular person. I'm telling you, Tyler, you're living on borrowed time. Beaver wants one thing. Revenge. He's not gonna sleep until he beats the crap out of you."

"Yeah, so?" I said, because I didn't know what else to say.

"So Beaver isn't the type to lose sleep. He'll be waiting for you after school." Lymie was talking real slow like he thought I was a foreigner or something.

"Yeah, so?" I said again.

"How can you stand there saying 'Yeah, so' like that?" Lymie threw up his arms in disgust. "Look, come home on my bus, and have Mrs. Saunders pick you up at my place."

"Naw, if he's gonna do something to me, I'd rather not have to wait around all week for it. Besides, I don't think he will." If I was trying to convince myself, it wasn't working.

"Suit yourself. But I've gotten kind of used to seeing your goofy face the way it is. And after Beaver gets done with you, I won't recognize it." He shook his head, tapped my shoulder, and left for class. Shoulder-tapping was pretty affectionate for Lymie. He must have been pretty worried.

As much as I hated to think about it, Lymie was right. The fact that I was so much smaller than Beaver probably made him all the madder, having to wear those cuts and bruises from somebody he could have killed if a teacher hadn't stopped him. I could still see Beaver's heartless eyes glaring at me from his bloody face, and

I got chills thinking about meeting that face and those eyes where there weren't any teachers or anybody around.

I spent the afternoon trying to think up a plan. Begging for mercy was tempting, but that was out. Even if I could bear the humiliation, Beaver would never buy it. He'd probably wait till I got done, and then slam his fist down my throat. And avoiding him was out. I couldn't avoid him forever unless I moved back to Los Angeles, and he might even come for me there, if someone told him where it was. And reasoning with him was out. Lymie was right about that. I might as well try to reason with a killer grizzly bear.

Every time a teacher called on me, Mary Grace jabbed me between the shoulder blades to snap me out of it. After our last class as we walked to our lockers, she asked me if I felt all right.

"You're really out of it, Tyler. How hard did you get hit?"

"Not very," I said. "I'm all right."

"I can't believe you fought that guy. You must be crazy."

"Gee, thanks, Mom."

"I'm serious. What if that gorilla is waiting for you after school?"

"I don't care," I said. "It's a free country."

"Macho isn't cool anymore, Tyler. Grow up. He's twice your size."

"Look," I told her. "I'm sorry. But what am I supposed to do? I've been thinking about it all afternoon. Believe me, I don't like getting beat up. But what do you want me to do, buy a gun?"

"Why don't you wait and go home with me after my history club meeting? Beaver'll be gone by then."

"No, I'll be all right." I didn't want to tell her about my allergy shot. I already felt like enough of a wimp.

"Well, at least you're a runner. You outran him once today and if he tries to grab you, you'll just have to do it again. After a while he's bound to cool down."

"I have a feeling the sun cools down faster than Beaver."

We finished putting our books in our lockers and taking out the ones we needed for the evening. Mary Grace automatically switched a couple on me as we talked. Then she looked me right in the eye.

"Promise me you'll be careful, Tyler. Can you at least do that?"

"I will. I'll be careful. Really."

She gave me a long, hard look, probably trying to remember me as I was. Then she turned and left for her meeting. I was alone. Surrounded by kids, but still alone.

As I left school, I could feel kids watching me, but I didn't feel good about it like I had earlier. I walked staring straight ahead, not looking at anyone. I know it's stupid, but I felt like I should be given a last meal or a last cigarette, even though I was too scared to eat, and I don't smoke. When I reached the corner of Main Street and headed down it toward Academy Park, I was sweating something fierce. And when I saw the crowd of kids milling around the fountain, a drop of icy sweat rolled down the inside of my arm. My legs felt rubbery, but I tried to look nonchalant, like a normal kid walking home after a normal day at school.

As I got closer, I saw that many of the kids were

older than me, high school kids. They watched me approach and some of them poked each other. All conversation stopped and they stood there, edgy and excited. What better way to end a day than by watching some scared kid get mauled. One of them yelled, "Get ready, Beaver. He looks real tough." He laughed and a few other kids joined in. The kid that spoke was Mark Blumberg, the principal's son. I'd seen him lots of times at Buster's. He and his goofy friend Jack used to hang around with BooBoo, but I couldn't figure out why. Mark was a lousy wise guy. The type of guy who got his kicks by watching people squirm. He was a junior and you'd think he would have gotten over that by now. He was smart, and mean, and I think I hated him worse than Beaver. At least Beaver was dumb.

Beaver pushed his way to the front of the group and stepped into my path. He pulled his shirt slowly over his head and handed it to Mark. He flexed his muscles and looked down at me with a smile that wasn't a smile at all. His shoulders were thick and well developed, but his stomach looked soft and paunchy like a beer drinker's. I stared at the dark hair which crept up to his navel. I thought foolishly that it wasn't fair for someone to beat me up who had hair around his navel. I stood frozen, waiting for something to happen.

"We got something to finish, don't we, rich boy?" He jerked his hand up and I flinched. A few kids laughed.

My mouth was dry and tasted like tin. I knew my voice would shake if I tried to speak, so I kept quiet, hoping Beaver wouldn't drag it out too long.

A sudden shift of Beaver's weight, and a punch flew at my head. I ducked and delivered a hard one with all of me behind it into the soft, hairy belly button. As I straightened up I heard almost before I felt a sickening thud on the top of my head. The force of it drove me backward into waiting arms which trampolined me back into the action. My hair was grabbed and my head was yanked back. A crushing forearm knocked through my upper body, and my head flopped forward until my jaw slammed my chest. The world sounded like it was under water. The side of my face was being hammered and I stumbled backward, no longer understanding what was happening to me. A knee slammed up under my ribs lifting me off my feet, and I felt something warm, almost hot, spreading over the insides of my icy cold legs. My bones seemed to rattle as my rear thumped the sidewalk. I lurched forward instinctively, jamming my head between my knees, and locking my fingers behind my ears. And I hid motionless over the sidewalk like a rabbit under the shadow of an eagle. Footsteps pounded past me. Almost from another world. I was distantly aware of one sharp kick in my side, and then all was silent.

I didn't move. For what seemed like a long time.

"Can you get up?"

I knew the gruff voice.

"Come on, Tyler. Get up and let me have a look at you."

Hands tried to rock my head back, and I locked my hands and knees all the tighter around it.

"Go away. Leave me alone, Chuckie. Please." I was crying now, and pleading.

"I'm bringing you home," he said. "I'm not leaving without you." As he spoke, he was firmly prying my knees down, tearing down the walls of my hideout.

"Chuckie, will you just get out of here!" I cried. "I pissed my pants. Why can't you leave me alone?" I was really sobbing now and my face burned with shame.

Chuckie pulled me to my feet and held my head from turning away as he examined my face and mouth. I could taste his fingers feeling around my teeth. Then he felt around my nose and wiped his snotty, bloody hand on his own tee shirt.

"Get in the car." When I didn't move, he pulled me, opened the door, and pushed me in. "Don't worry about the seat. You're not that wet."

He got in the other side, and I collapsed forward with my shame into my old retreat. I wished I'd never have to face Chuckie again in my whole life.

"Looks like you took quite a beating."

I didn't answer.

"But you did all right this morning, huh?"

That almost made me look up. I wondered how he knew about that.

"I ran into Mr. Johnson in the diner at noon," he said, stepping on the gas. "You're a gutsy kid. Not too sensible, maybe, but gutsy. I'll say that for you."

I felt the car pull into my long driveway. Drops of water from the sprinklers spattered the hood and windshield. Chuckie stopped the car, and I peeked up out the windshield. Mrs. Saunders and two old neighbor ladies were sitting on the porch, watching us and talking. I looked down at the dark splotches of dampness on my light blue corduroys. I lowered my head to my knees again and prayed I'd disappear.

"Come on." Chuckie got out. I heard my door swing open, but I didn't budge.

"Come on, hothead! You ought to know better than

to be fighting.'' Chuckie was talking loud, and he hardly ever talked loud. He wrenched me from the car. In my misery I tried weakly to shake loose from his grip, to keep from having to walk past those ladies with wet pants.

"A kid that's a hothead needs to be cooled down. Then maybe he can think straight." Picking me up by the neck and the seat of my pants, Chuckie hoisted me over the nearest sprinkler. Cold water stung my face, and I struggled clumsily to kick and punch my way free. Chuckie laughed and kept waving me over the sprinkler. I wanted to kill him.

"Chuckie, have you lost your mind? Put him down!" Mrs. Saunders yelled from the porch.

Chuckie yanked up on my neck, and swung me to my feet. He couldn't let go of me completely because I was still kicking and punching like a wild man. Mrs. Saunders came tearing down the porch steps but froze in her tracks when she got a look at me.

"Tyler, what in the world . . ."

I stopped struggling and looked from her bewildered face to down at myself. I could only imagine what my face looked like, but my shirt and pants were streaked with blood, and more thin watery blood still dribbled from my nose and chin down my front. I was soaked from head to toe.

"Tyler, you poor . . . What in . . . Chuckie, how could . . ." Mrs. Saunders didn't know whether to examine me or hug me, so she did a little of both. Plus she tried to pry me away from Chuckie.

"He needed to be cooled down, that's all. He's all right now." Chuckie looked at me and winked. And I suddenly realized with a burst of joy that my pants were no longer any wetter than the rest of me. Chuckie smiled and pulled my arm. "Come on, tough guy. Let's get you inside and cleaned up."

Mrs. Saunders yanked me back, and looked at Chuckie the way you'd look at a mad dog.

"It's all right, Mrs. Saunders," I said, smiling. "It worked. I feel a lot better now."

As Chuckie led me up the porch steps, he stopped for a second and nodded politely to the ladies.

"Good afternoon, ladies. Lovely day."

Their jaws flopped down and their eyes widened at the sight of me. Chuckie pushed me into the house before they could say anything.

And that was how I came to adopt Chuckie Deegan into my family.

# VIII

It took about fifteen minutes of holding my head back before my nose stopped bleeding. By then my whole face felt stiff, and I talked through clenched teeth because it hurt to move my jaw. My teeth felt like they'd all been jarred loose, and my bruised ribs hurt if I breathed too hard. And I noticed I was a little lightheaded whenever I sat up. But it felt good to be in clean, dry clothes, and it was a relief to know that some terrible ordeal was behind me, kind of like the way I used to feel when I was little and walking out of the dentist's office.

Chuckie had shooed Mrs. Saunders out of my room after watching five minutes of her yelling and shaking her finger at me, and then hugging me and thanking God I was all right, over and over. He told her to call the doctor's office and tell them I'd be a little late for my appointment. He even said he'd drive me, which Mrs. Saunders wasn't crazy about at first, but she finally said all right. Driving through cities made her nervous, and she knew we wouldn't get home till after dark.

"Chuckie?" My voice sounded funny sneaking out from behind my teeth.

"What do you need now, Ace?"

I sat up and watched him rocking back in the chair he'd pulled up next to my bed.

"Thanks, Chuckie . . . I really mean it." It sounded stupid, but I didn't know how else to start. And I really did mean it.

"What for? I brought you home. Big deal."

"You know what I mean. When you found me, I was sitting on the sidewalk crying like a baby. I wanted to . . . I don't know . . . melt into the sidewalk or something. And you . . . you know . . . you chased everybody away and brought me home. If any of those kids had ever known I wet my pants, I swear I never would have gone back to that school. Ever. And then when we got home, you got yelled at for holding me over the sprinkler, just so I wouldn't be humiliated in front of Mrs. Saunders's friends."

"You can thank Mrs. Saunders for my showing up when I did. She sent me to get you. And as for the sprinkler deal, that was a last minute thought. You looked like you could use a good rinse." He pushed my head back again and pried the pillow under my shoulders. "Keep that head back until we're sure the bleeding has stopped. If you had a dipstick in your head, we'd probably find you were already down a quart."

"I couldn't help it," I said to the ceiling. "About my pants, I mean. He slammed me so hard I didn't even know where I was. It's not like I was being a baby or something. I usually don't even cry."

"No big deal. Don't worry about it."

"Chuckie?"

70

"Yeah?"

"Tell me about something stupid you did." I was up on my elbows now.

"What are you talking about? Who said I did anything stupid?"

"Whenever I feel really bad about something embarrassing or idiotic I've done, Chris always tells me a story about something embarrassing or idiotic he did. Then I don't feel so bad."

"Come on, Tyler, get out of here. He's your brother. He's supposed to do stuff like that." He pushed my head back.

"Yeah, but he's not here," I said. "Come on. It'll be fun."

"The next time somebody asks me to tell something stupid I did, I'll be able to tell them about being in this conversation."

"So will you do it?"

"Well, you could at least give me a minute to think," Chuckie said. "Would that be asking too much? I can't come up with something right on the spur of the moment."

"That's all right," I said. "Take your time. But remember, it has to be something so bad that even after years have gone by, you still think back and cringe because you're still so ashamed." My head popped up to study Chuckie's face.

"All right. Let me see . . . okay, I've got it. This one's bad." He pushed my head back and giggled. I'd never heard Chuckie giggle before. "This is just between us, right?"

"Yeah, and if I tell, you can tell how I pissed my pants." Now I was giggling. I tried to stop because it made my face and my ribs hurt.

71

"All right. Good enough. Now listen." Chuckie leaned forward and talked low, like we were sitting around a campfire or something. "You know how when you're in high school and taking driver ed., you have to watch these films about safety on the road? Well, I guess you wouldn't know about that yet. But anyway, in order to make you a more careful driver, they always show you these films about high school kids drinking, and driving too fast on their way to a prom or some-place."

"I know," I said.

"What do you mean, you know?"

"Chris took driver ed. and he told me."

"That's wonderful. Now shut up and listen."

"Sorry."

"Now where was I? Oh, yeah. At the beginning of the movie, you meet all the kids and see them making plans for the big day, you know, the prom or whatever. And you meet their parents and families, and you're supposed to think how these kids and their parents are like you and your parents and everybody."

"Did you?" My head popped up.

"Did I what?"

"Did you think how the kids were like you and your parents and everybody?"

"How do I know? Yeah, I guess I did. But that's beside the point. Now will you shut up and listen?"

"Sorry. But I thought that might be important."

"It's not, so shut up and listen. If something is im-portant, I'll tell you." He pushed my head back, harder this time.

"Sorry," I said. "Go ahead."

Chuckie looked at me a minute to make sure I was done.

"Okay, so you're supposed to identify with these kids. But the thing is, you always know they're going to get into this awful, gruesome accident on the way to the prom, or wherever it is they're going."

I knew all that from Christopher, but I thought I'd better keep quiet.

"And so on the day we all know we're going to see one of these films, all the boys start bugging the girls, telling them how bloody and grisly the film's going to be, you know, to get them going. And the girls scream and carry on about how they won't be able to look, or how they'll have to leave. You follow me so far?"

"Yeah, I bet this is gonna be good."

"Sure, good for you. I'm the jerk in this story."

"Well, come on. Shut up and tell it."

"All right, keep your shirt on. So we get there, into the driver ed. room, and all the boys, myself included, are acting cool and telling the girls to make sure they get good seats so they won't miss any of the blood and gore. And the teacher tells everybody to shut up because he's been hearing the same stuff all day, and he turns the projector on. We watch about twenty minutes and get to know everybody in the film, and then we start poking the girls because we know the good part's coming. The kids are all in a convertible whizzing down the highway, drinking beer and having the time of their lives. Only they don't see this tractor trailer truck stopped right in front of them with the lights flashing, so they hit it, dead on. By now the girls in the class are going hysterical, but this is only the beginning. Now they start mixing in footage of a real accident just like the one they set you up for. And you see real kids, some of them are dead, and mangled, and twisted into funny shapes on the highway, and some of them are alive and screaming for help. Then they show the parents, the actor parents, of one of the dead kids and they're saying how they hope their kid is having a good time. The camera goes back to the scene of the accident, the real accident, and shows close-ups of this mangled dead kid. And that's as far as I got.''

''You ralphed?''

''I what?''

''Ralphed. You know, upchucked, barfed.''

''Whose story is this, Ace? Yeah, I did. All over my desk. It was right after lunch, and believe me, it was a gusher. And what made it worse was that the girl I was sitting behind and poking earlier in the film had this beautiful, long blonde hair trailing over my desk. What a mess! All I can remember is girls screaming, especially that one girl with the blonde hair. And I took off.''

''Yeeooow! Whoooa, that must have been awful!''

''Yeah, I'll never forget it. I wanted to disappear from the face of the earth. And it's like you said. I still cringe when I think about that.''

''I threw up when I was watching *The Exorcist*,'' I said. ''Chris had a whole bunch of his friends over and we were all sitting around our living room munching out, when the girl that was possessed threw up this green goop and it sprayed right out into the priest's face. And I threw up all over the couch. Mom was really mad at Chris for letting me watch that movie. I was only eight or nine then. Plus, the couch was brand new.''

''Now look what you've done,'' Chuckie said. ''I spend all that time telling you a humiliating story so you'll feel better, and then you go and try to match it. Now you're one up on me.'' He laughed.

"That's my problem. I'm not even thirteen, and I've already experienced more humiliation than most adults. Probably every humiliating experience you can mention, I can match."

We were both laughing like total fools now. My face felt like it would crack, and my ribs were in agony.

"Go ahead, Chuckie. Try again," I said. "CHUCKIE DEEGAN, THIS IS YOUR HUMILIATING LIFE!" I tried to sound like that TV announcer on "This is Your Life." We were in stitches, and boy did I hurt.

Finally Chuckie said we'd better get going or I'd never make my appointment. He promised to tell me more grimy, mortifying details about his life on the way to the doctor's. We hurried down the stairs and out onto the porch. I still felt light-headed and rubbery-kneed from the beating, and when I saw the two old neighbor ladies sitting there staring at me with that same amazed look they were wearing an hour before, I burst out laughing all over again, and I couldn't have stopped if you put a gun to my head. I can only imagine how ridiculous I must have looked with a swollen nose and a bruised and cut-up face, clutching my sides with the pain of trying to stifle myself. And to top it off, when I laugh real hard, I make a shrill, squealy kind of noise that Chris says sounds like a nail being pulled out of a board.

Chuckie wasn't any better. He grabbed my arm and dragged me down the steps and tossed me into the car. But as I watched him through the windshield heading for his side of the car, the whole thing struck him as funny again, and he doubled over in front of the hood and disappeared until his door popped open and he crawled in behind the wheel. We took off before Mrs.

Saunders had a chance to change her mind. I have to admit, we probably didn't look that sane.

It's hard to believe that anybody who was as miserable as I was that afternoon could have had as good a time as I did that evening. Chuckie and I shared some more cringe material, and we were still laughing when we got to Albany. I figured nobody could have more shame buried in their systems than we did. Except maybe Christopher. He had some pretty bad stories too.

As it turned out, the doctor wouldn't even give me my shot. One look at me and he said to forget it. With the kind of shape I was in, he was afraid the shot would send me into allergic shock or something. After he checked me all over, he gave me some kind of oral medication to take until I came back the next week.

"Oh, and by the way," he said smiling, "No driving. These pills might make you drowsy. And, hey, next time pick on somebody your own size."

For dinner I dragged Chuckie into this little health-food restaurant on Washington Avenue, even though he was afraid he'd have to end up eating tofu and sprouts. Chuckie handed me a *Times Union* he'd grabbed and told me to find something good to do. I love movies more than anybody I know and was heading for that section when I spotted an ad for this championship wrestling show at the RPI Fieldhouse in Troy. I'd seen a lot of wrestling on TV, but I'd never been to a live show before. Chuckie wasn't too keen on the idea (I think he was afraid somebody'd see him there), but he'd made the offer so he was stuck. We called Mrs. Saunders so she wouldn't worry about us.

We were lucky to get tickets. Even though it was a weeknight, the place was packed. The show was pretty much what you'd expect, a lot of fake kicks and punches, and a lot of fake interviews and arguments, and guys chasing each other with chairs and tables, and the bad guys whipping sharp things out of their trunks that everybody in the crowd could see, but the ref couldn't. But I have to admit it was pretty entertaining. I even saw Chuckie laughing a few times.

One thing that always gets me about professional wrestling is the crowd. You notice it on TV, but when you're right there with them, it's incredible. You have to wonder where they dig up some of these people. I swear they really thought this was real life. And I'm not talking about the little kids. I'm talking about full grown adults and old ladies and stuff. I made the mistake one time of cheering for the bad guy and booing for the good guy, just to be funny, and this old lady turned around and started swearing at me, and a bunch of other people started shaking their fists at me. Chuckie poked me and told me to shut up, but I was about ready to shut up on my own anyway. I couldn't believe it.

And it's like the promoters of the show knew what kind of junk the crowd would go crazy for, and they really fed it to them. Like there were these two bad guys who were on the same tag team. One of them was supposed to be some kind of sheik in this big turban, and the other was this humongous bald-headed guy who was supposed to be a Russian, or a Mongolian or something, although Chuckie said he'd give me ten to one neither of them had ever been out of this country. The guy who was supposedly the Russian or whatever made a big deal out of standing up there in the ring and trying to sing his national anthem while the sheik was running around the ring and yelling at everybody to stand up.

That made the crowd go really nuts. I mean totally bonkers. There were crazies all around us wrapping themselves up in American flags, screaming their lungs out, and shaking their fists. They weren't kidding either. Groups from all over the fieldhouse started singing "The Star-Spangled Banner" for all they were worth. People were almost knocking themselves out trying to drown out this guy's singing on the P.A. system. I couldn't believe it. Half this crowd would have probably been willing to drop bombs on Russian cities or someplace over that stupid song. And the funny thing was the stupid guy singing it was probably from Detroit or someplace.

To add fuel to the fire, the guys they were supposed to be fighting were supposed to stand for The American Way or something. They looked real clean cut, and you could tell at a glance they were the type of guys who respected women and spent their free time visiting crippled kids in the hospital. Another thing you could tell at a glance was that these guys hated loudmouthed sheiks in turbans, not to mention foreigners singing their national anthem in our country, worse than the crowd, if that was possible. The crowd could hardly stand it when they chased the Russian and the sheik away from the mike and started singing "My Country 'Tis of Thee." If I'd ever booed during that song, I'd have been dead meat.

Later, in the car, I asked Chuckie why he thought the crowd fell for the whole routine.

"I don't know, Ace. But I bet if I did, I'd know why there were wars, and terrorism, and cruelty, the whole works. Maybe it's like . . . I don't know . . . People like to feel that they're one of the good guys, and the easiest way to do that is to create bad guys and hate them and fight them. That probably doesn't make much sense to you, does it?"

"Yeah, it does," I said. "That's kind of like the reason why Mom can't stand most politicians. She says instead of trying to make the country better they just keep making speeches about how great we already are. Like we're better than everybody else."

"Hey, people eat that stuff up, Ace. It makes them feel like winners."

Chuckie pulled the car onto the interstate. I was quiet for a minute, thinking.

"Chuckie?"

"Yeah."

"You know how I went to this prep school for a few months?"

"What about it?"

"When I first got there, I roomed with this real fat kid. The poor guy. He had acne real bad, he was lousy at sports, he didn't have any personality . . . I don't know . . . He didn't have anything going for him at all. He wasn't even smart. And it seemed like the whole school ganged up on that guy. They did awful stuff to him."

Chuckie nodded but didn't say anything. He kept his eyes on the road.

"Chuckie?"

"Yeah, Ace?"

"Would you have stuck up for him?"

He waited a while before answering.

"I don't know. That's a tough one. It'd be easy to say yes, but if you're actually there . . ."

"I bet you would have."

That was the last either of us said for a while. The

subject was getting kind of depressing, and I was getting too sleepy to do much more thinking anyway. I slumped back in my seat and let my mind go blank, concentrating on feeling the vibrations from the road. Just as I was about three-quarters drifted off, a strange thought hit me from nowhere, like they do sometimes. I popped up with a start.

"Hey, Chuckie. Didn't you say that Mrs. Saunders sent you to bring me home from school?"

"Yeah, Ace. Why?"

"I always walk home alone," I said. "How did she know I was going to get beat up?"

"She didn't."

"Then why'd you have to come get me?" I shielded my eyes from the glare of oncoming traffic.

"I wasn't going to tell you this, but I suppose you'll hear about it soon enough anyway."

"What? Come on, Chuckie. You can tell me."

"It's about BooBoo Anderson. The coroner says he didn't drown out at the quarry. The water in his lungs was chlorinated. You know, like water in a pool. Somebody dumped him in the quarry after he was dead. And what he died from was a broken neck. He'd been struck in the head so hard that his neck snapped. Nobody knows much yet, but those gossipy ladies got Mrs. Saunders all shook up by talking about murder and everything, and she was afraid to have you walking home alone."

This was news. And to think Lymie and I may have been at the quarry right when the murderers were there!

Suddenly I was wide awake again.

# IX

IT WAS ALMOST 11:00 before I got to school on
Wednesday. I never even heard my alarm. Because
we got home so late, Mrs. Saunders came in and flicked
it off without waking me. She told me afterward that
she really thought I needed my sleep, especially since
Chuckie had told her the pills I was taking might make
me extra tired.

Before I could go to any classes, I had to bring my
note to the nurse's office and get an admittance slip.
The nurse was busy arguing with some kid who claimed
he had a headache and wanted to go home. He told her
there was something about math class that always gave
him a headache, and that somebody ought to check that
classroom for chemical contamination. The nurse looked
like she'd heard it all before.

"Back to class, Harvey. If you die at your desk over
a long division problem, I'll take complete responsibility."

Harvey groaned and turned toward the door. When
he saw me standing there, he said, "I hope you're not
planning on leaving."

81

The nurse took my note, read it, and looked up at me.

"Got home late from a wrestling show?" she said. "From the looks of it, you must have been sitting a little too close to the ring."

I laughed, remembering my cuts and bruises.

"I got in a fight with a kid after school yesterday."

"A fight, huh," she said through her teeth, the way I was talking. "I hope you lost."

When I looked confused, she said, "If you didn't lose, I'd hate to treat the guy who did."

I laughed again. She was pretty funny.

"I didn't see much of the other kid," I said. "But I think he's all right."

This time she laughed. Then she asked me a few questions to make sure nobody at home was beating me or anything. I told her Mrs. Saunders was too old to hit me even if she wanted to, and that Chuckie was the one who had saved me from getting beat up worse than I did. She seemed convinced and wrote me an admittance slip.

"You know, Tyler," she said as I was leaving, "being tired is not exactly a legal excuse, but I have to admit it's more honest than a lot of the excuses I'm expected to swallow. See that it doesn't happen again."

The bell rang just as I stepped into the hall. And Mary Grace was at her locker when I got there.

"Tyler, thank God. You're in one piece," she said. "I was going crazy! Yesterday I called your house to see if you made it home all right, and a lady there told me you were still at the doctor's. Well, that was bad enough, but this morning when you didn't show up, I really got scared. Some of the kids said you'd been

82

practically beaten into the sidewalk." As Mary Grace spoke, she was at it again, digging out the books I'd need for the rest of the day.

I explained about my allergy shots in Albany.

"Only the doctor wouldn't give me the shot anyway because he said I was too wracked up."

"He's got that right. You're a mess."

"I'm fine," I told her. "Today I just overslept."

"Well, one good thing came out of this," Mary Grace said. "I don't think Beaver will bother you anymore. When you didn't show up this morning, Beaver was afraid you were crippled or in a coma or something."

"I'm surprised he cared."

"He didn't, except that he thought the police might be coming for him. And I told him I hoped they did. I almost spit in his face."

It was funny picturing someone like Mary Grace standing up to a thug like Beaver. And I couldn't picture her spitting on even a sidewalk.

My next class turned out to be lunch. Mary Grace was on B lunch so she headed for home ec. Since Mrs. Saunders had made me eat breakfast, I wasn't hungry, but I went to the cafeteria and tried to do some of the homework I was supposed to do the night before. I had barely opened up my social studies book when an overloaded tray slid toward me, splashing milk all over my book, and Lymie plopped down in front of me.

"He lives! T. Tyler McAllister has survived the deadliest ordeal known to man, an encounter with a mad Beaver!" He paused a second to gawk at my face. "And he only looks a little funnier than he used to."

Lymie was shoveling lunch into his face almost before his rear end hit the seat.

"Lymie, you clod. Look what you did to my book!"

"Couldn't be helped," Lymie said. "I thought I was seeing a ghost." He continued shoveling as I grabbed a couple of napkins off his tray and dried off my pages as much as I could.

"I warned you, Tyler. You never listen to me, but I told you what would happen."

"Yeah, well, if I had listened to you, I'd still be looking over my shoulder every time I took a step. At least now it's over."

"But if you listened to me, you'd be able to open your mouth a little when you talked." He imitated the way I was talking through my teeth.

"Maybe we should get Beaver to smack *you* so you'll learn to keep your mouth closed when you eat."

"Funny, Ty, you're a regular barrel of laughs, you are," Lymie said. "Hey, did you hear the news? You know, about BooBoo. It might've been murder like you said." He crammed half a roll into his mouth. A little thing like murder wasn't enough to keep Lymie from stuffing his face.

"I heard," I said, closing my book. "What do you think, Lymie? What do you make of it?"

"Who knows? BooBoo's mother told the cops that the last she saw BooBoo, he was headed down the street to Mark Blumberg's house. He used to hang around there a lot. But Mark said he never got there."

"Somehow I can't picture Mark Blumberg being nice to somebody like BooBoo. That kid's sick." I remembered how excited he got at the prospect of me getting beat up.

84

"Yeah, he's a sick puppy, that's for sure," Lymie said. "But who ever said he was nice to BooBoo? He and that geek Jack Robbins used to drag BooBoo around with them, but it wasn't because they were such good guys. They'd always boss him around and laugh at him if he did anything dumb. And the rotten thing was, BooBoo really thought they were his friends."

"That stinks. Why didn't anybody tell BooBoo?"

"Would you want to be the one to tell somebody that his best friends didn't even like him?"

"I see what you mean." I shook my head. Mark was an even bigger jerk than I thought. "So, Lymie, if BooBoo didn't show up at Mark's house, where'd he go?"

"According to Mark and Jack, they were both sitting on Mark's front porch about the time BooBoo was supposed to have left his house. And they noticed these two grubby looking hitchhikers walking up the street toward BooBoo's house. Only they didn't think anything of it at the time until afterward when the police questioned them, and they found out BooBoo was supposed to have showed up."

"So the police think the hitchhikers murdered BooBoo?"

"No, Tyler, you goofball, they think my grandmother did it. Duh. That's why they're running around questioning everybody trying to get more information on these guys."

"Boy, Lymie," I said, "this is really spooky. Any of us could have met them on the street that day." I tried to think what I'd do if two guys tried to grab me.

"You're telling me! A lot of kids saw them."

Lymie was right. For the rest of the afternoon everybody was talking about those two hitchhikers, and it seemed like almost everybody had seen them. If they were all telling the truth, which I doubt, those poor guys must have hitchhiked up and down every street in the village, and then headed out and crisscrossed most of the surrounding countryside. Some of the kids said the guys looked like hippies (they still used that term in Wakefield), and some said they were two seedy-looking old guys. Not only that, but it seemed like every time they were spotted, their hair color changed and they were wearing different clothes.

By seventh period I had lost interest in all the stories. Those pills the doctor gave me were really catching up to me, and probably like Chuckie said, I didn't have as much blood left in me as I was supposed to have. I felt like one of those guys in the movies who's had some kind of knockout powder put in his drink. I thought about going home, but the nurse had already made it clear that tiredness wasn't a good enough excuse for getting out of school, and I wasn't up for sneaking out. Besides, there was only one period left. I figured it shouldn't be too hard to get through one period.

Old Lady Waverly passed out one of her famous worksheets on the three basic kinds of rocks, which we were supposed to have read about in Chapter 3 the night before. Luckily it was open book because I hadn't read it, and rocks aren't really my thing anyway. But I'm a fast reader, and I used the index to find the page numbers, and then skimmed paragraphs looking for key words. The work was easy, but pretty boring, and being as tired as I was, it was pretty hard for me to keep my eyes open. I had told Mary Grace about the pills before class, so whenever my head started to droop down, she jabbed me in the back with her pen.

Old Lady Waverly sat up at her desk giving everybody the evil eye, and every so often she'd go up and down the aisles on patrol or something, making sure kids were being quiet and neat, in that order. Any kind of noise tended to bring out the worst in her. She must have had ears like a dog. And sometimes she'd stop and wad up a kid's paper saying, "Is this what you call neat?" Last week Jason Rounds got thrown out for saying, "Not anymore."

It didn't take much to rub Old Lady Waverly the wrong way.

I worked on, silently, and as neat as I could manage, jotting down information on igneous rocks, and volcanoes, and sedimentary . . . riverbeds . . . metamorphic . . . The fluorescent lights overhead buzzed monotonously. I felt another jab and straightened up.

"Mary Grace!" The whole class snapped to attention. Old Lady Waverly paused and took a few steps toward us. "Perhaps you should have brought a cattle prod to school. Then maybe you'd have to wake our friend less frequently. But today, since you don't seem to have the proper equipment, why don't you move to the front of the room."

Mary Grace grabbed her stuff and moved to an empty seat in the front. I went back to work. Old Lady Waverly's smiling face didn't fool anybody. Everybody knew she didn't have a real sense of humor. When she joked around, that only meant she was like a half a millimeter away from flying totally off the handle.

As I stared at the book, I could feel her eyes beading into my skull. It seemed like forever before I heard the

slow footsteps which meant she had resumed her
rounds. At least then I could relax and breathe again.
Whew. I don't know why she didn't like me. Was
sleeping that terrible a crime? At least it was quiet. I
didn't snore or anything. It probably wasn't only me.
She probably didn't like anybody. Even a goody-two-
shoes like Mary Grace. Rocks. They were about the
only thing she liked. Somebody like Old Lady Waverly
probably had them stuck all around her house. Like pet
rocks or something. She probably even talked to them.
It wouldn't surprise me. But I bet she hated rock music. Because that was normal. I couldn't wait to get
home. I'd go up to my room, find a good album, put
on my headphones, and melt into my bed. Just melt
away . . . not a worry in the world . . . that'd be nice
. . . real nice . . .

# X

"IT IS MOST unfortunate, Mr. McAllister, that you persist on using Mrs. Waverly's class as your personal napping center. You may have surmised that Mrs. Waverly does not take kindly to the notion of her room being used as a rest stop on the freeway of public education." Mr. Blumberg leaned forward in his chair, planted his elbows firmly on his desk, and peered over his glasses at me. He looked as tired as I was, but that didn't seem to be helping me any.

A yawn was struggling to come up out of me. I fought it back by clenching my jaw while the rest of my face worked at keeping my eyes propped open. My lungs sucked in air loudly through my teeth with a couple of hitching gasps, and my eyes watered, blurring Mr. Blumberg's attempt at a smile. I blinked hard to wipe my vision clear and nodded my head although I wasn't really sure what he said. A chill had crept into my bones. Air always seems colder and damper when you wake up too fast. And Mr. Blumberg sure didn't warm the room up any.

"I notice from the attendance sheet that you arrived late this morning," Mr. Blumberg continued, holding up the paper. His other hand waved the little paper that I recognized as my note. It was a regular show and tell. "I took the liberty of checking your excuse and found that the reason for your tardiness was that you attended a professional wrestling show." He said professional wrestling slowly, in a voice dripping with scorn, like I must be some kind of lowlife to go to something like that. He even held the note away from his face between his thumb and his forefinger like it was probably swimming with germs.

"We didn't get home till after midnight," I said, because Mr. Blumberg didn't say anything more. "Mrs. Saunders thought I needed more sleep." I knew how lame that sounded. I was hoping he'd yell at me quick and tell me to get lost. No such luck.

"Mr. McAllister, forgive me for questioning the priorities of your household, but certainly you must understand that one of the purposes of a school is to foster a sense of responsibility in its students. In all its students. You do understand that, don't you?" He filed the attendance sheet and dropped my note.

"Yeah . . . yes."

"Perhaps. But I sometimes find that students who come from—how shall I put it—families with more modern notions, as it were, sometimes suffer from a kind of benign neglect. I find this especially true among the more affluent. They develop little awareness of consequences." Mr. Blumberg folded his hands, leaned back in his chair, and regarded me thoughtfully, giving me time for his words to sink in. Which didn't do a bit of good, seeing how I had no idea what he was talking about.

"I didn't mean to fall asleep on Mrs. Waverly, Mr.

90

Blumberg," I said, because I can't stand silence when I'm in trouble. "I told her I was sorry."

"Let's simply say that showing up late for school with an unacceptable excuse, and falling asleep on Mrs. Waverly, as you so colorfully put it, seems to say something about your general attitude toward our educational establishment. I trust you didn't fall asleep at the . . . show." He spit out "show" like it was a dirty word, and he looked at me like I was a lowlife again.

"I wasn't tired then." Sometimes I hate listening to myself.

"Of course," he said, and he closed his eyes, pulled off his glasses, and rubbed the bridge of his nose. He looked like he might be fighting off a wicked headache. "I also understand you were fighting in gym class yesterday." He put the glasses back on. "Mr. Johnson didn't see fit to file a report, but I generally find out things that happen in my school."

His school. I thought of his son, Mark, who was probably not only a sicko, but a tattletale too. I didn't say anything.

"From the looks of you, it must have been quite a fight."

"Most of these I didn't get till after school," I said, feeling my cuts and bruises. "Why don't you ask your son? He was there."

I think I sounded nastier than I meant to. You could see Mr. Blumberg stiffen up.

"That my son had the misfortune to happen upon a senseless fight is hardly pertinent. What is pertinent is that you seem to have a history of fighting. It is true, is it not, that you were expelled from a previous school for fighting?"

91

"Not really expelled," I said, squirming in my seat. "They just said that I probably shouldn't come back."

"You have quite a knack for euphemisms, my young friend." Mr. Blumberg's voice was meaner now. It was stupid of me to have brought up his son. "Tell me, Mr. McAllister, are you planning to carry on this pugilistic tradition here at Wakefield?"

"No." I hung my head. And I didn't even know what "pugilistic tradition" meant.

"I would like," Mr. Blumberg continued, "to have this . . . er . . . Mrs. Saunders, I believe her name is, come in to have a talk with me. I'm assuming that your mother is, shall we say, preoccupied with work and not available."

"She's in Colombia."

"Yes, I seem to have heard that." He shook his head, picked up the phone, and began to dial my number. He rapped a pencil impatiently on his desk, waiting, but no one answered. He hung up the phone and looked at me like he was puzzled. I was relieved. Maybe he'd only send me home with a nasty note this time.

"Tell me, Mr. McAllister. Are you left unsupervised much of the time?" He stared at me thoughtfully.

"Not really," I said. "I'm supervised almost all the time. Mrs. Saunders is probably out getting groceries or something."

Mr. Blumberg kept on staring at me, not saying anything.

"And even if she does have to leave," I said, "she tells Chuckie—he's our groundskeeper—to look after me."

Mr. Blumberg straightened up, and his face became less rigid. He looked like a TV detective who had stumbled onto an important clue. I knew what he was thinking.

"Your mother is out of the country. Your housekeeper is obviously out of the house. And I'm to understand that your groundskeeper will, as you put it, look after you." He paused and studied me a moment before continuing. I could almost detect a trace of kindness and concern in his face. "Tell me, son, how do you feel about this? Don't you ever wish your mother could be at home with you?"

"Yeah, I guess," I said. "But Mrs. Saunders is like family. Besides, my mom will be home the first chance she gets. It's not that bad. Really." I hated the idea of him thinking I was some kind of abandoned child, tossed from person to person with no one really taking care of me. It wasn't like that at all.

"Mr. McAllister, I'd like you to wait in the internal suspension room next to my office until I'm able to contact your maid. I don't like the idea of sending a child home to an empty house. And since your mother has chosen . . . well, let's just say we'll wait until I've made contact."

Mr. Blumberg led me down the narrow hallway that connected the main office to the guidance office, his hand on my shoulder the whole way. I think the guy really felt sorry for me. He guided me into a small room filled with two rows of desks, the kind they have in libraries that wrap around you with big sides so you can't see the kid next to you without leaning back.

"Choose a desk, Mr. McAllister, and make yourself at home. This will be a good chance for you to start on your homework, wouldn't you say? Do you need anything from your locker?"

"No, I've got stuff to work on. Thanks," I said, holding up my books.

"Very well then. I'll let you know when I've contacted your maid."

Mr. Blumberg left and I was alone in that creepy, quiet room. I headed for the farthest desk in the back corner, hidden from the door and nice and private, but with a good window view. Turning my chair to the window, I put my feet up on the sill and rocked back and forth, thinking. Thinking about how I always get myself into trouble without even trying. I was hardly into my second week of school and already Mrs. Saunders was being dragged in to have to listen to Mr. Blumberg tell her what he thought my problem was. Which made me mad at first, seeing how he'd raised a kid like Mark. But the thing was, it wasn't just Mr. Blumberg. I couldn't very well blame him for all my problems. He didn't give me allergies . . . or asthma attacks . . . or sleeping attacks. And he didn't get me kicked out of my last school. That was all stuff that happened without any help from him. Maybe I was a born loser, some kind of unfixable lemon doomed to screw up, no matter what. Besides running, school was the only thing I was halfway decent in, but lately I couldn't even do that right. Maybe I was born under a bad star or something. Maybe I was nothing more than a skinny version of Ralph Waller.

Waller was the kid I was assigned to room with when I first got to Grant Academy. He was this huge mass of blubber and the kids all called him "Waller the Whale" and "Waller the Whopper" and stuff. I didn't call him anything. I was too depressed. Dad had put me on a bus right after Easter vacation when he'd finally convinced Mom to give boarding school a shot. He said it would toughen me up and be the best thing in the world for me. When I got there, I didn't cry, but I had this sick feeling in the pit of my stomach, and I didn't feel much like talking to anybody. It felt like that dream I used to have had come true, the one where I fell off the edge of the world and was stranded completely alone. That didn't bother Waller any. He didn't seem to want to talk anyway.

At breakfast the first morning, some of the guys told me I'd better ask for a transfer unless I wanted to be stuck with Waller the rest of the year. The thing was, Waller was sitting right there listening, and they didn't even seem to care. I didn't know what to say. I ended up telling them Waller was all right, and I didn't mind staying with him, figuring maybe I could get a transfer later without making him feel so bad. The guys looked at me like I was crazy.

Maybe nobody ever stuck up for Waller before. I don't know. All I know is Waller became my shadow after that. He walked with me to class, he ate lunch with me, then dinner, and then he followed me back to the dorm, only stopping first at the candy machine to fill his pockets. Exactly what he needed.

I was miserable. As if I didn't already feel bad enough, being so homesick I could barely keep from bursting into tears, and I had to put up with the loneliness of being with Waller. The guys all hooted and jeered whenever he walked by them, and he'd slink away after me. He never even said anything back to them.

On the second night some guys came barging into our room about an hour after dinner. Six of them, all a few years older than me, and dressed perfectly in their blue uniforms with black stripes and spotless shiny black shoes. They ignored me at my desk and zeroed in on Waller. I recognized the one who seemed to be in charge as the kid who carried the flag in the flag-raising ceremony that morning. He cuffed Waller a few times before he spoke, his voice hissing with hatred. "How's it going, Fat Boy?" Another slap. "Did you miss us, Waller, buddy?" Another slap. Harder each time. A few other boys moved in and jabbed him in the side.

Waller turned away, whimpering and huddling over his desk. I started to get up, but what I saw next stopped me in my tracks. I couldn't believe my eyes. Waller's shaky hands began to open his candy, shielding it with his body and peeking sideways the way a hungry dog does when it finds food and doesn't want to share. It was horrible . . . revolting to watch. He started stuffing candy into his face. And at that moment I learned something. I learned that I hated Waller almost as much as the other guys did. I hated him for all the misery he stood for. And I hated the other boys for the cruelty they stood for. And I hated my room. And I hated the whole stupid lousy school for dragging me away from home. I hated my allergies. I hated how lonely I was, how helpless. I hated so much that tears started streaming down my face, and I slumped back into my chair.

The kid from the flag-raising ceremony struck Waller hard on the side of the head, and he rolled heavily from his chair to the floor like a plastic bag filled with guts. He was whining and still clutching his candy. The other kids kicked him as he writhed like a fat worm, curling up around his candy.

The seething, hissing threats that followed the jabs

nd kicks, and Waller's whimpering cries rose in my
ead until my head seemed to expand with them like a
alloon. I clutched my ears to stop the noise, but it
idn't stop. It got louder. I got up and yelled at them
o cut it out, and they laughed and kicked Waller some
nore. I screamed at them to get out, and one of them
nocked me down. My arms grabbed a chair and started
vhaling kids with it. I heard smashing sounds and
creaming, my own maybe. Arms and bodies crushed
ne into my bed, and punched me, and crammed a pil-
ow in my face. The next thing I knew, the housemaster
vas dragging me downstairs. He'd had to practically
ry the chair out of my hands.

I might as well have left that night, because that was
he beginning of the end of my stay at Grant Academy.
Two long months and I don't know how many fights
ater, I came home for the summer. I'd lost ten pounds,
nd I was ten times more miserable than before I left
ome. That was the summer I was so sick. That was
he summer my father died.

Chris told me afterward that I should be proud that I
tuck up for Waller. But the truth is, I didn't. I knew I
lidn't.

I jumped when the dismissal bell went off. Pretty
soon the happy sounds of kids heading for freedom came
in through my window. I watched sadly as kids laughed
and poked one another, hopping on buses and zooming
down the aisles to get the best seats. The town kids
filed down the sidewalk in little groups heading for Main
Street. I wanted to join them more than anything.

The door behind me clicked and I sat up, expecting
to hear Mr. Blumberg saying I could go home too. But
the door banged closed and for a moment I thought I

97

was alone again. Then I heard a voice right behind my wrap-around desk.

"Well, what do you think?" I knew that voice.

"I don't like it. I told you I didn't like it from the start." That voice didn't quite ring a bell.

"Relax. We answered their questions, didn't we? It's over, so forget it."

"We throw BooBoo into the quarry, and you tell me to forget it!"

"Shut up about that!"

"And what about the hitchhikers? The cops asked too many questions."

I held my breath as my ears strained to hear their hoarse whispers.

"Good for them. They asked the questions and we answered them." He laughed, the same nasty, sneery laugh I heard the day before when he told Beaver I looked tough. "And Jack, the thing that really cracks me up is that *we* didn't even see any hitchhikers, but everybody else did!"

"I'm glad you're happy," Jack said. "Me, I haven't slept right since before this whole mess."

The door clicked open again. I must have been about purple now from holding my breath. I prayed they were leaving.

"What are you boys doing here?" Mr. Blumberg's stern, no-nonsense voice.

"Waiting for you, Dad. You were on the phone. I need your car keys. We have to pick up some stuff at Jack's house. How about it?"

"I suppose so," Mr. Blumberg said. "I'll get them for you in a minute. But see that you go straight there and straight back . . . Now where did that boy go? Mr.

McAllister, are you in here?'' His voice moved in on my hideout behind the row of desks. I was still frozen up against the back of my chair. "Ah, there you are. I was afraid you'd fallen asleep again. You're free to go now. I'll meet with you and Mrs. Saunders tomorrow at two. And, might I suggest that you go to bed early tonight?''

He gave me one of those grim, principal looks, but his face seemed to soften when he saw how spooked I was. He put his hand on my shoulder and walked me out the door. Glancing back down the narrow hallway, I saw Mark Blumberg and Jack Robbins staring at me, looking like they'd just seen a ghost.

Which is what I was afraid I'd end up being if they got their hands on me.

# XI

I'VE NEVER BEEN a very decisive kid. At least that's what Chris always tells me. He used to get a kick out of me when we'd be in New York or someplace and we had to cross a busy street. I'd stand there swiveling my head back and forth, waiting for just the right moment to make my move. I'd always make a couple of false starts and then hop back up on the curb. Chris would look at me and shake his head. Then he'd clamp his hand around my arm, and exactly at the right moment, he'd give a yank and off we'd go, zipping through an opening in traffic. No hesitation. No false starts. No sweat. We're different like that.

And if a kid has trouble deciding when to cross a street, you can just imagine how he'd react knowing he was the only one to know about some kind of murder cover-up. And to make matters worse, I knew they knew I knew.

I hurried down the sidewalk toward Main Street, too scared to even look behind me. I wondered what Mark and Jack would do to me. They might even kill me. Stranger things have happened. But waiting and not knowing was what scared me the most. If they didn't do something soon, I might die of fear.

A big black car pulled up next to me and the door popped open.

"Hey, McAllister, get in!"

Jack's voice shook and his face looked pinched. He jumped out of the passenger side not three feet from me, and I could see the car's red interior. I bolted before I even knew it. Running is the one thing my body understands and does well. I had zipped down a driveway and cleared a fence before my brain even caught on. A man yelled at me from his backyard, and his voice trailed off in the distance. I should have stopped. He was big and mean-looking with a face like a bulldog. Angry maybe, like people get at kids, but not a killer. I should have stopped. He could have protected me.

I poured on more steam and pumped hard, in case Jack was right on my heels. I was gasping for breath. You can only sprint for so long. When I made it to the cemetery behind our property, I glanced behind me and saw that I was alone. I wasn't all out sprinting now, but I was still moving at a pretty good clip. I stayed clear of the lanes, figuring I could outrun Mark and Jack if I had to, but not their car. My foot snagged a low marker hidden in the grass, and I sprawled to my hands and knees, but scrambled back to my feet without losing any time. It wasn't till then that I noticed I was still clutching the bookbag Mrs. Saunders had dug out of my closet for me. It was just as well. If somebody grabbed me, I could always whale him a good one with it. But I prayed it wouldn't come to that.

Leaving the cemetery at a slow jog, I cut through a narrow pine woods. I could see my house now, but instead of feeling relief, it gave me the creeps. Mark and Jack would count on my coming home, and might be waiting for me. I threw my bookbag over our black iron fence and kept my eyes peeled as I rolled over it. The sharp points jabbed into my legs and I felt my pants rip.

Dashing across the open lawn, I made it to Chuckie's cottage. I beat on the door so hard, it's a wonder the glass didn't pop out. I waited, hearing only the sound of my own wheezing, and then beat on it some more. No one answered. How would I protect myself and Mrs. Saunders if Chuckie wasn't around?

I ran past the main house, chucked my bookbag on the porch steps, and headed for the garage. Both doors were locked. I paced back and forth in front of the garage like expectant fathers always do in the movies. Thinking. Or more like trying to think. It isn't easy coming up with something when you're looking over your shoulder and jumping at every little sound. After a minute, I darted back to the house.

As I fumbled for my keys, I glanced over my shoulder down the long driveway. What I saw made my eyes almost pop out of their sockets. The big, black car was rolling to a stop in front of our entrance archway. When the door opened and Jack jumped out, my heart nearly stopped. Jamming the key in the latch, I flung myself at the door, slammed it shut, and double locked it. Me, who always got yelled at for never remembering to lock anything. I even flipped the switch to the burglar alarm which Mom had had installed, the one Chris and I teased her about because we never figured crime was too big in a place like Wakefield. I was grateful for it now. If anyone tried to open a door or a first floor window, a loud siren would go off in the house and down at the police station. Mrs. Saunders never left it on in the daytime because I was always setting it off by accident.

Dropping my bookbag, I darted into the den because it had a big bay window jutting out from the house that would give me a wider range of vision as to what was going on in the front yard. I sneaked the curtains back and peeked out, holding my breath and hoping I didn't come face to face with Mark's blistering, beady eyes. The big car was still out front, but the door was closed and Mark and Jack were both inside. From the way their heads bobbed around and the way Jack kept jerking his thumb toward the house, it looked like they were having a pretty lively discussion. Finally, Jack slumped down in the seat with his head in his hands, and the car rolled slowly down the street and out of sight.

I wondered what they might have decided. And what I should do. I remembered how Mom used to tell me how Mrs. Saunders had kind of a bad heart and that I should help her out whenever I could and lift heavy things for her and stuff like that. So I couldn't very well run up to an old lady with a bad heart and tell her there were two murderers stalking the place.

The door to the den snapped open, and I nearly jumped out the window and left my skin behind the way a snake does.

"Tyler, I thought I heard you come in."

"Whew! Mrs. Saunders," I said. "You scared me."

"You're as white as a ghost. Are you sure you feel all right?" She came over and started feeling my head like she always does.

"I'm all right," I said, trying to smile and look healthy.

"Why, you're all overheated." She stepped back and studied me. "And what in the world happened to those pants?"

"I kinda jogged home. And I ripped these climbing our fence."

"Tyler, is that bully after you again?"

"Naw, I think he learned his lesson." I laughed weakly. "You heard about me falling asleep?"

"Yes, I heard." Mrs. Saunders sighed and smoothed my hair back.

"Are you mad?"

"No, I'm not *mad*," she said, giving me a hug. "I know you're trying to do your best. That's all we ask."

"I'm trying," I told her, "I really am. But things . . . happen to me. I don't know. I mean, it's not like I decided to go to science class and fall asleep or something."

"I know, dear. Don't worry. I'm sure those pills you're taking didn't help any. We'll straighten it all out with Mr. Blumberg tomorrow."

"I think he thinks there's something wrong with me," I said. "He brought up about Grant Academy and said how I had a history of fighting."

"Well, there's not, and you don't," Mrs. Saunders said, suddenly bristling. "And you needn't take things people say too seriously. You're too sensitive sometimes for your own good."

"I think he thinks I'm a psychopath or something."

"A psychopath! Don't be ridiculous. You're a thoughtful, well-mannered boy. I only wish you could have heard Chuckie talking about you today. Chuckie, who doesn't usually say two words. He went on and on. It sounded like you two really hit it off after all these weeks."

"Where is Chuckie?" I asked, casually, I hoped. "I looked for him outside."

"Don't you remember, honey? Today was the day

104

for him to drive to New York and pick up some new things your mother ordered for the house. He won't be back until tomorrow afternoon."

"Oh, no!" I moaned before I even realized it. "Not today of all days."

"He'll be back before you know it." She paused and gave me the eye, the one adults give you when they think you're hiding something. "Was there something you needed him for, dear?"

"Naw, I guess not," I said. "There was something I wanted to tell him is all."

"Well, you can tell him tomorrow, and I know he'll be glad to listen. Come on. I'll get you a snack. And don't forget it's time for your medication. Remember, three times a day until your shot next week." She shooed me toward the kitchen.

"I'm not really hungry, thanks. And I'm starting to think those pills are more trouble than they're worth."

"Not if they keep you from having an asthma attack," she said. "Relax, dear. We'll deal with Mr. Blumberg tomorrow. Don't be so . . . what's the word you kids use . . . so uptight."

I didn't know anybody my age who said uptight, but I didn't say anything. I tried to look pleasant as I swallowed my pills, which wasn't easy considering my brain was whirling with thoughts of murder—both BooBoo's and the possibility of my own. I kept picturing myself as a chalk outline on the carpet. Mrs. Saunders was studying me pretty close, and she looked a little worried herself. She took another temperature check on my forehead, and then started feeling around my neck for signs of disease.

"You don't have a fever, but you seem so jumpy.

Have you been eating sweets?'' She stepped back and regarded me thoughtfully.

"No, Mrs. Saunders, I didn't eat anything since you fed me. I'm all right. I feel great.'' I was lying. I felt all shivery and weak-kneed.

"Why don't you run up to your room and get your homework done? Then tonight you can watch a little TV and get to bed early for a change. I don't like the way you look lately.'' She kissed me on the forehead.

Upstairs I paced around my room, back and forth about fifty thousand times, trying to decide what to do. I thought about calling the police, but why should they believe me? Not that many people around town knew me, and I didn't have any proof of anything. Also, being in trouble with the principal and reporting that his son was a murderer wouldn't look so good. Plus, if I did that, Mr. Blumberg would be sure to drag out my school records for everybody and his brother to see, so they'd think I was some kind of dirtbag who shouldn't be believed anyway. So much for calling the police.

Then I thought about calling Chris because he's always good in an emergency. I called and got the answering machine, which was Chris's voice saying he'd be out until tomorrow and to leave a short message. What I had to say I couldn't say to a machine.

And it wouldn't be any use to call Lymie. He'd be out doing chores. I could ride my bike to his place, but I didn't dare. I'd be a sitting duck pedaling along the side of the road. Besides, Lymie was only a kid like me anyway. How much protection could he be?

Like I said, I'm not a very decisive kid.

I moped around my room for an hour or so, unable to keep my mind on my homework. What did homework matter when I might not be around long enough to turn it in? I slumped back on my bed in misery. Why me? Why always me? I couldn't understand it. It seemed sometimes that my whole life, and especially the last few years, had been so jinxed that hardly anything went right for me. I was allergic to what seemed like half the things on the face of the earth. I had been thrown out of a school, and then only after nearly dying of loneliness. I didn't have a father, and when I did, he couldn't seem to figure me out anyway. And when Mom bought a new house, mainly for me, to give me a chance to start a new life, the bad luck followed me across the country. Sneaking out at night and going swimming, a thing that millions of kids must have done, for me turns into a disaster. Who but me would be jinxed enough to swim into a dead body? And even if they were, what would be the chances of them overhearing the body's murderers talking about it? The whole thing even sounded ridiculous. It didn't seem fair.

I wished I could be one of those people who had their lives organized and who always seemed to know exactly where they were going. No fear. No sweat. No stupid blunders. Mom was like that. In addition to her acting and reading scripts and planning film projects, she managed to do all kinds of public service things like benefits for clean air and water and rain forests and stuff. And even with all the trouble I'd been for her, she was always able to bounce back and stay on top of everything. And Chris. He was making a big name for himself and never seemed to be afraid or lonely or confused. And Chuckie. He had this quiet confident way of facing life and taking things in stride. I couldn't picture him lying around his room shaking in his boots the way I was. Even Mary Grace, a kid who was my own age, had all the ins and outs of school down pat and was always prepared for whatever might happen.

Not me. I was a lemon if ever there was one. A textbook case, clear and simple. If Mom had bought me at a store instead of giving birth to me, she could have exchanged me for a kid who worked better.

"Excuse me, sir. I have a complaint. I bought my last son here, and he's been a perfect joy. But this one is a different story. Nothing but problems. You should be ashamed of yourselves for selling such a lemon to a good customer."

"Please accept my humblest apologies, Ms. LaMar. Of course, I can see at a glance that this child is defective. You must understand that no matter how careful we are, these things do happen. Please, choose any child in the store, compliments of the house. Maybe you'd like a nice musical prodigy? Or maybe our Olympic model? That's been a big seller this year."

"To tell you the truth, at this point I'll settle for one who can breathe on his own and stay out of trouble for more than a day at a time."

Of course, I was being unfair. Mom would never do that. She'd keep worrying herself sick about me and sinking more money into doctor bills and hospital bills and new houses so I'd have a better environment and all that. And every time she got me back on my feet, I'd use those feet to rush into my next disaster. But Mom was loyal. And she really did love me. But let's face it. How long can you love a lemon?

# XII

THE PHONE NEXT to my bed rang and I jumped. I looked at my clock. It was nearly 5:00. My history book lay open on my chest. Why would I go to bed with my history book and with all my clothes still on? And why wasn't it dark? The phone stopped ringing and I lay there trying to remember.

"Tyler, honey, it's for you!" Mrs. Saunders, yelling from downstairs.

I rolled toward the phone, and my history book fell to the floor with a thud. I rubbed my head and stared at the phone, not too sure what to do with it. Wait. It wasn't five in the morning. I must have fallen asleep after school. And with a sickening wave I remembered Mark and Jack and all the trouble I was in.

"Hullow."

"Tyler, is that you? I can barely hear you." The cheerful voice sounded familiar, but I couldn't remember who it belonged to.

"Yeah . . . ziz . . . Tyler," I mumbled. I don't wake up fast.

"Tyler, you sound like you're dying. I waited for . . ."

"Whoziss?"

"Tyler, are you all right? This is Mary Grace. I waited for you after school, but you didn't show up."

"Oh, yeah. I didn't . . . I just woke up." Even in my stupor it was good to hear her happy voice.

"I didn't mean to bother you, but I wanted to know if you got in much trouble."

"Uh, well . . . give me a second." I sat up and tried to rub some life into my head.

"You know you sleep more than my nephew does, and he's only two."

"Thanks, Mary Grace," I said. "You're gonna give me a hard time about that too? I told you about the pills. I can't help it."

"Tyler, I'm sorry. I was only teasing. I called because I was worried about you."

"It's not your fault. I'm just being sensitive. That's another of my many problems." I knew I sounded like a jerk, but that's what I felt like.

"Boy, what's with you today?" Mary Grace said. "Did you get in that much trouble? I mean, sleeping in school isn't that serious, is it? Actually it's probably the only sensible thing to do in one of Old Lady Waverly's classes. Let's face it, if her worksheets get any duller, they'll have to start serving coffee in her room."

I smiled. Almost.

"No, I'm not in that much trouble. Mrs. Saunders and I have to meet with Mr. Blumberg tomorrow. It shouldn't be too big a deal."

"Okay, good. So what's bothering you?"

I waited for a minute, thinking.

"Mary Grace, if I told you something, something really important, would you promise never to breathe a word of it to anybody? Ever?"

"Tyler, you're scaring me. Are you in some kind of real trouble?"

"Promise?"

"All right, all right. I promise. Should I be sitting down or something?"

"I can't tell you on the phone. I've gotta tell you in person. It's a long story. Can I come over tonight?"

"Yeah, of course you can. Look, why don't you come over right now and have dinner with us?"

"I can't. It's got to be dark. It'd be too risky in the daylight."

"Tyler!" She almost shouted. "Don't do this to me. You're really scaring me! Look, why don't I send my father over right now to pick you up?"

"No, that's all right. I'll see you sometime after eight. Don't worry. I'm just a dramatic kid. It runs in the family. Get it?" I forced a tiny chuckle.

"I hope you're right," she told me.

At dinner I told Mrs. Saunders that I had to go over to Mary Grace's and get help on math. I'm a lousy liar, and if she'd really looked me in the eye, she would have known something was fishy. She didn't notice my guilty face, but she still wasn't crazy about the idea of my leaving, what with the whole BooBoo thing unsolved, and me needing extra sleep because of the pills. Plus, she was still worried about my seeming so jumpy.

"Tyler, you turned on the alarm, didn't you?"

"I happened to think of it."

"You never thought of it before."

"Maybe I'm getting more responsible."

She was studying me close-up, but that line cracked her up. She finally said I could go but only after she cranked my head around till we were eye to eye and told me if I wasn't home by 9:30 and in bed by 10:00, I'd have some real worries.

I waited till it was pretty dark before I dared leave the house. I'd been running around upstairs since dinner, peeking out the windows, making sure I didn't see anything suspicious around the yard. The coast seemed clear. I told Mrs. Saunders to turn the alarm back on after I left, and that got her going again, and she almost locked me up for the night. I told her I wouldn't talk to strangers and I could outrun almost anybody on foot, and she gave in again. By this time, I was having second thoughts about leaving myself.

It was a breezy night and darker than I thought it would be. I crept around behind the house, looking around and listening. I couldn't really hear much because there was quite a breeze whizzing past my ears, and until my eyes adjusted, I couldn't see anything either. I didn't look forward to walking through the dark woods or the cemetery alone, but if Jack and Mark were looking for me, it would probably be right on the streets.

I headed toward the iron fence, steering clear of any trees or bushes big enough for anybody to hide behind. I stopped at the fence and looked around to make sure I wasn't being followed. The back of the house was dark and its roofline and sides were outlined by the glow of streetlights. I shuddered. It would have been easy for someone to have seen me leaving the house and be sneaking up on me right now. It was stupid of me to wait until dark. In the daytime at least you could see danger coming. Even the air felt creepy at night.

I climbed the fence without ripping my pants this time and started through the pine woods. It was too dark o run. I could make out the outlines of the big trees, but I was afraid of poking my eye out on one of the little jagged branches that hung down around my head. The pine needles cushioned my footsteps, and I seemed to glide slowly over the ground. Sometimes when I turned around to check behind me, a twig would rub against the back of my neck and my skin would crawl and my hair would feel like it was trying to climb off the top of my head. I knew that if someone had been lurking at the edge of the woods watching me leave the house, I'd be walking right into a trap. Maybe I should have taken the street. At least then I'd be able to take off like a shot and scream my lungs out if I had to. If I got mangled in the woods, no one would hear a thing. It might even be days before anyone found me.

I moved faster, holding my arms out to protect my eyes, but it still took forever to get to the end of that little woods. The cemetery was easier to manage once I found the lane, but a cemetery is a creepy place to be alone in at night, especially when your skin is already all creepy and goosebumpy. I jogged down the lane slowly, being careful not to twist my ankle on a rock or a stick. My pace picked up as I saw the silhouetted shapes of the houses on Main Street.

I hopped the picket fence into the bulldog-face guy's backyard. A real dog barked and the backyard light snapped on. I dropped flat on my face in a shadow on the dewy grass and prayed the guy wouldn't let the dog out. It didn't sound like the type of dog that wanted to play. I also prayed that snakes didn't come out at night since I hate snakes even in the daytime. Peeking up, I saw the bulldog guy's face at the back door looking right at me but not seeing me. Growling at his dog to shut up, he flicked off the light and his hulklike shape moved off through the blue glow of a TV set in the next room. I bolted down his driveway like a rocket, turned onto Main Street, and poured on the steam for all I was worth. Mary Grace's house was only a little more than a quarter mile away, but after coming this far, I didn't want to take any chances.

I was pretty well winded by the time I scrambled up the steps of Mary Grace's front porch. I hit the glowing orange button once and turned to check the street. I didn't see anybody, but when the porch light snapped on, I felt like I was in the spotlight at Carnegie Hall. I whirled around and scrunched up against the door. When the door opened I almost jumped over the top of the lady inside. Mrs. Madigan, I figured. She looked down at me kind of surprised, and then yelled up to Mary Grace that her "little friend" was here. Smiling, she led me into the living room where Mr. Madigan sat reading the paper.

"You poor dear," she said, still looking at me kind of funny, "you look like you ran the whole way."

Mr. Madigan stood up to shake my hand. He was a big guy, graying at the temples, and he had one of those grips where you could almost feel your bones cracking. He was about to offer me a seat when Mary Grace yelled for me to come upstairs.

"Nice to meet you," I gasped and headed for the staircase. It was a relief not to have to sit in a small, quiet living room making wheezing noises in front of somebody's parents I didn't even know yet.

Mary Grace met me at the top of the stairs, dragged me into her room, and slammed the door like I was a slave on the underground railroad or something.

114

"Door!" we heard Mr. Madigan yell from downstairs, and Mary Grace ran back and opened the door. That's all I needed, to get beat up by some girl's father.

"Tyler," Mary Grace started in, "I'm going crazy! Tell me what's the matter!" She looked down at my clothes. "Why do you have wet grass all over the front of you? And why are you all out of breath?"

"I'm lucky . . . that's all I got . . . lying around . . . in some guy's yard . . . that owns a big dog," I said, still gasping for air.

"Sit down," she told me. "Relax. I'll get you a glass of water. If you keel over and die, I'll never get the story."

It was difficult for me to get started. I didn't know where to begin. So I started with Lymie and me sneaking out of the house last Saturday and went on from there. Mary Grace stopped me a few times to ask about this or that, but no matter what I said she didn't act like I was crazy or the victim of an overactive imagination or something. And she really listened to everything I said. Before I knew it, I had told her not only about BooBoo and Mark and Jack, but also about Christopher and Mom, and Mrs. Saunders, and Chuckie, and Grant Academy. I even told her how Dad would be mad if he were around and heard me spilling my guts because he thought boys were supposed to keep things inside and work them out privately, and never in front of females. And I told him how Mom always defended me against Dad, telling him all the time that he was left over from the Dark Ages and that guys didn't have to be like that any more and to get off my back. I'd never said anything out loud about Mom and Dad's fights before, I guess because deep down inside me, I felt responsible for them not getting along and finally getting a divorce. I couldn't tell Mom this because I knew how much it would upset her, and I realized after telling the whole story to Mary Grace that I had been afraid to say anything to Chris because I was worried that somewhere deep down inside, he thought I was to blame too, although he'd never say it.

I must have gone on for at least an hour. When I realized how self-centered I'd been, dominating the whole conversation with my problems, I was kind of embarrassed and started to apologize all over the place.

"Hey, don't apologize," Mary Grace said. "Do you realize that in one evening I've gotten to know you, really, more than I've gotten to know any of the other kids I've gone through school with for eight years? It's amazing. I mean, think about it. How many times do you get a chance to really talk to somebody, you know, without all the little games and cover-ups and everything? You're crazy if you think I'm going to let you apologize for that."

"But I didn't give you a chance to say hardly anything."

"Tonight you had things to say. Maybe next time I'll have things I want to say, and I'll know I've got you."

I couldn't believe Mary Grace was my age, or Lymie's. And I didn't have to worry about her rushing to school the next day and nearly breaking her neck to blab all the personal stuff I'd told her to her friends. I knew I didn't.

"Right now, Tyler, let's get back to Mark and Jack. I think you're wrong about them."

"Mary Grace, I'm telling you. I heard them. I wasn't dreaming. They killed BooBoo."

116

Mary Grace shook her head.

"Think about what you really heard. Nobody actually said anything about murder. I've known Mark Blumberg all my life. His father's good friends with my father. And I know Mark can be mean, and he can be selfish, and he can be stupid, but I can't see him as a murderer. He and Jack are covering up something, but probably not murder."

That made sense. A little anyway.

"But why did they try to get me into their car, and why did they go to my house? They didn't exactly look like they wanted to take me out for ice cream."

"That's the way Mark is, and probably Jack's the same way. He intimidates people to get what he wants. And believe me, Mark's used to getting what he wants. And now he wants something from you. If you got into that car, Mark would have threatened you, probably, and maybe even hit you, but I doubt it. He wants you quiet, but he also saw you take a pretty bad beating without backing down. And you said yourself how Jack looked scared. I bet neither of them knew what they wanted to do with you. Maybe they only wanted to talk to you to see if they could find some angle to get through to you. But I think you're safe. Mark will never make citizen of the year, but I'd bet anything he's not a killer. And I don't think Jack does anything without Mark's stamp of approval."

I felt a little better hearing that. After all, Mary Grace knew Mark a lot better than I did.

The phone rang downstairs and Mrs. Madigan yelled up to me. I looked at the clock. It was almost ten. Mrs. Madigan told me that Mrs. Saunders was going crazy worrying because I should have been home by now. Mr. Madigan said he'd drive me.

Mrs. Saunders was waiting for me on the front porch. She didn't look pleased. I scooted up the steps and into the house. I didn't even look over my shoulder for Mark and Jack.

# XIII

"YOU TOLD! I don't believe it. We had a deal, and the first pretty face that comes along you blab your guts out to. I don't believe it!"

Lymie grunted and puffed his way around the track. Beaver never needed to worry about Lymie winning his way to captain. I jogged backwards trying to explain, but Lymie wouldn't even look at me. His head was down, his eyes following the white line. I couldn't blame him really. I *had* promised to keep my mouth shut.

"Lymie, can't you get it through your thick head? I thought they might kill me or something. You're afraid you might get grounded for a week. I thought I was gonna be put in the ground. Forever! Besides, Mary Grace promised she wouldn't say anything."

"Oh, sure, like a girl can be counted on to keep her mouth shut. You're a guy and you couldn't even keep quiet."

"Good thinking, Lyme. Real modern."

"I don't want to be modern, Tyler. I want to stay out of trouble, and I thought I could count on you. I was wrong."

119

"Come on, Lyme. PLEASE?" I begged. I hate it when people are disappointed in me. I really hate it. "Come on, Lyme. You can at least look at me, can't you? PLEASE?"

Lymie continued to puff around the track without even raising his head. I was going crazy. Here was my best friend and he couldn't even stand to look at me. He thought I was some kind of traitor or something. I had to make him listen. I had to do something. Almost before *I* knew it, let alone Lymie, I stopped, jammed my foot in front of Lymie's, yanked his arm and rolled to the side. As he pitched forward and toppled to the ground, I rolled on top of him, pinning his shoulders down with my knees.

"Tyler, you butthead, get off of me! I'll kill you! I really will!" Lymie flopped around the ground like a madman in the middle of some kind of fit. He almost flung me off a couple of times. I don't weigh all that much and Lymie was pretty strong.

"Lymie, don't make me get rough," I told him as I jammed my knees hard as I could into his shoulders. " 'Cause I'll belt you if I have to. Mrs. Saunders is about ready to kill me after last night, and I can't stand it if you're mad at me too. What do you want me to say? I'm sorry. I was scared. I didn't know what to do. Is that a crime?" So much had happened to me so fast over the last few days I was afraid I was going to start crying all over the place.

Suddenly Lymie stopped struggling beneath me, and I felt him begin to shake. With laughter. The stupid fool was laughing at me. The laughter grew until he was choking and teary-eyed, and it was making me madder by the minute. I didn't see anything funny going on. I leaned up and ground all the weight I had into his shoulders.

"What's so funny, jerkface?" I yelled.

"You . . . you are . . ." He was so out of breath from running and laughing he could barely get the words out. "You . . . you crack me up . . . 'Don't make me get rough.' When you get serious . . . you're the funniest kid I know. Eeeoooowwww! Get your bony knees off me. They're liable to cut me." This sent him into another round of convulsions. "You look so goofy when you try to be serious . . . You crack me up . . . Eeeoooowwww . . . I'll kill you . . ."

I had to laugh, too, after a while because Lymie looked pretty goofy himself, but I didn't miss the opportunity to get a couple more knee jabs in, seeing how Lymie was nearly paralyzed.

"You boys want to be alone?" Mr. Johnson's rough voice startled us, and we both hopped to our feet and started jogging again without waiting to see if he had anything else to say. When we got out of Mr. Johnson's range, I turned to Lymie, and when his eyes met mine, he cracked up all over again.

"Lymie, don't be such a jerk. You think because you're stronger than me that's all there is. I could dazzle you with my speed." I cuffed him lightly on the side of the head a few times to demonstrate, and backpedaled out beyond his reach. "Attack and retreat. That's how I can get you. No sweat at all."

"You better hope you can run forever, Tyler," Lymie panted, "because when I get my hands on you, you know I can mash you into a bloody pulp. No sweat at all."

"Good for you, Lymie. The whole universe is proud

of you. I'm trying to talk serious here and first you act like a big baby, and now you're a tough guy."

"Oh, I like the way you explain things, Ty. I don't call it being a baby when you're mad at somebody for breaking a promise. And I wasn't being a tough guy. I was stating facts."

"Fine, Lymie. Great. You're tough. But what I want to know is what should we do?"

"We? Did I hear you say 'we'? Those guys weren't chasing me around in a car, Tyler. I don't know where you get this 'we' stuff."

I wasn't in the mood for listening to Lymie's whole song and dance routine. Not today.

"Cut the crap, Lymie. You're supposed to be my friend. Besides, you know as much as I do now."

"Yeah, thanks to you. Come to think of it, it's thanks to you we found the body in the first place. I'm telling you, you're an accident waiting to happen."

"Tell me about it," I said. We had finished our laps and were walking to the football field.

"Look, Tyler, I know you're upset and worried and everything, but there's nothing we can do. Let's just see what happens. If you go squealing to the cops or somebody without any evidence, you'll end up looking like a total fool. Mark and Jack will deny everything and that'll be that."

"How about you though? Won't you back me up?"

"Back you up with what? What do I know?"

"You were at the quarry when we found the body. And you saw two people in a car with a red interior, same as Blumberg's."

"Hold the phone, butt-for-brains, you want to get me grounded for that lousy information? We've been through this before. There must be millions of cars with red interiors.''

He saw how disappointed I was.

''Really, Ty, I don't see that our saying anything will make any difference.''

We walked quietly for a while, thinking.

''Well, I feel funny about not saying anything. It doesn't seem right.''

''All's I'm asking you to do is to can it for a while. At least for now.'' He stopped and looked at me. ''Just don't do anything stupid. For your sake as well as mine. Just keep your cool and we'll see what happens. You don't want to get all beat up again, do you? Huh, buddy, do you hear me?'' He rapped his knuckles on the side of my head.

''I hear you,'' I said. I heard him, but it didn't go down easy. I couldn't help feeling we owed BooBoo something, but maybe Lymie was right. It wouldn't hurt to wait a few days.

Most of the kids had finished their laps by the time we joined the group, and they were already picking up teams. Beaver was captain again, along with Ralph, so things were pretty much back to normal.

''Hey, McAllister,'' Beaver yelled, ''you're on my team. We can use your speed.''

My heart sank, wondering what Beaver had in store for me this time. As if I didn't have enough on my mind. I trudged over to join the team, watching Beaver suspiciously to see if there was a catch. He seemed friendly enough, at least as friendly as someone like Beaver ever got. He stepped in front of me as I approached.

''Hey, McAllister.'' He paused, shuffling his feet and

groping for the right words. "I was glad to see you in school yesterday. You know, that you weren't really hurt or nothing. I gotta admit, you got guts. You're pretty stupid, maybe, but you do got guts."

"Thanks," I said, trying not to sound sarcastic. I knew a lot of Beaver's change of heart was because he was so happy that he didn't get arrested or sued or something. But I also knew how hard it must have been for him to say what he said, especially in front of everybody. This didn't make him Mother Teresa or anything, but I did appreciate it.

"Hey, Beav?"

He turned and looked a little uncomfortable, like he was afraid I was going to wise off to him and start the whole thing over again.

"What?"

"Can we have Lymie on our team too?"

Beaver gave me a funny look. You could tell he wasn't used to taking requests, and it threw him off for a second.

"All right," he said. "He can be center. I'll be quarterback. And you'll be going out for passes." He turned to where Lymie was. "You," he told him, "over here."

Lymie came trotting over and stood next to me. After Beaver finished picking the rest of his team, he turned and glared down at the two of us.

"We better win," he said. And then with one finger on my chest and one finger on Lymie's chest, he pushed us out of his way.

Lymie and I looked at each other and kind of smiled to show how we weren't all that scared. But I swear to God, neither of us ever played harder in our lives.

# XIV

$\mathbf{M}$RS. SAUNDERS STARED straight ahead. She hadn't seen me come around the corner past the secretaries in the main office. I stopped for a second and watched her sitting there alone outside the principal's door. She looked tired and troubled, clutching her purse nervously, as if she'd done something wrong instead of me. If she'd known I was there, she would have perked up right away. The few times I'd seen Mrs. Saunders looking that worried were when she didn't know I was around. I felt pretty terrible about her getting dragged into the whole mess. She was old, probably sixty-five or so, not to mention her heart condition. She deserved better than to be sweating it out in front of some principal's office wondering how she'd be able to defend some dumb kid who had a habit of snoozing his way through science.

I started toward her again, deliberately squeaking my sneakers on the linoleum so she'd know I was there. She looked over and smiled, motioning me to sit in the empty chair next to her. All trace of worry had vanished from her face, and I wondered where it had gone.

"Are you still mad?" Selfish question. I should have asked her how she was.

"Mad is what dogs get, Tyler. You want to know if I'm still angry."

"Are you?"

"No, dear, I'm not angry. I just have to remind myself from time to time that you're a typical twelve-year-old boy, and your head is tied up with typical twelve-year-old boy things."

"Almost thirteen," I said glumly, "and I'm not sure all the things I do are so typical. I'm really sorry you got dragged into this."

"Don't you worry about me," she said, patting my knee. "I've been around long enough to be able to take care of myself. You're probably too young to remember, but I had to see a few teachers and principals for Christopher too."

"No kidding. I don't remember Chris ever getting into trouble." It was kind of nice to think that I wasn't the only one that messed up.

"Your brother was a good boy, same as you, but he wasn't perfect either, not by a long shot. He got into his share of fights like boys will, and believe me, he could be filled with the devil when he wanted to be." She thought for a minute. "Come to think of it, science wasn't his strongest area either. I remember one time he and a friend sneaked into the science room right before their earth science lab practical. Those two rascals went through all the rocks they were supposed to know how to identify, and figured they'd do better on the test if they threw all the ones they didn't know out the window. And believe me, they didn't know many of them." She nodded her head and smiled as she remembered. "He was a year older than you are now, Tyler, and in the ninth grade, as I recall it. The two of them might have gotten away with their funny business, except it was lunchtime and the entire faculty, including their science teacher, heard those rocks pinging off the sidewalk right outside the faculty room.'' She stopped and laughed, and I smiled, trying to picture the whole thing. ''There's not much you do, Tyler, that doesn't ring a bell with me about something Christopher did. But I'll say this for the two of you, and this is the God's honest truth, I've never known either of you to be anything but good when it came to the big things, the things that really matter.''

''Wow, that's a pretty neat story. Chris never told me that.''

''I suppose he figured you could come up with enough devilry without him supplying you with ideas. And I probably shouldn't be telling you this either, except . . .'' She paused and studied me a minute. ''Sometimes I think you take things too seriously, as if you think you're the only boy in the world who isn't perfect.''

''I'm not trying to be perfect, Mrs. Saunders. I just want to be normal. You know, like everybody else.''

''Oh, Tyler, can't you see there's a million ways to be normal? Christopher was normal in his way, and you're normal in yours. And you're both special. All I'm trying to say in my own clumsy way is that you should never think of yourself as a bother or a burden to any of us. You bring a lot of joy to us, Tyler, just the way you are. Your mother knows it, and your brother, and, as tough as your father was on you, I hope you realize you were something special to him too.''

I wanted to jump right up and hug her on the spot, but I didn't. It was amazing sometimes how she could tell what I was thinking and say the things I needed to hear. Mom and Chris were like that, too. I guess I was more like Dad in that respect. We both had trouble with saying the right thing at the right time.

The door opened and Mr. Blumberg stood there, shoulders back, hands on his vest, looking as if anything he might say would be the most important thing in the world. I remembered Lymie saying how I was funniest when I was the most serious. Now I knew what he meant. Mr. Blumberg did look pretty funny standing there all smug and important, especially considering he was going to be yelling at me for snoozing in class.

"Mrs. Saunders, I presume . . . and Tyler, please step into my office and have a seat."

He made this big sweeping gesture with his hand, and we jumped up and did like he said. He followed us in and sat behind his desk, regarding us thoughtfully and giving us time to soak up the importance of the occasion. Neither of us spoke. We just gawked back at him, so he cleared his throat and started in.

"I'm glad to have the opportunity to meet with both of you. I thought maybe if we had a chance to . . . to interact, we might be able to iron out what I perceive to be some difficulties."

He wanted to discuss my problems. Which we knew before he said anything.

"This interaction may prove valuable in preventing us from having to face more grave predicaments somewhere down the line." He waved his hand toward the window, like he thought maybe this predicament would take place in the parking lot.

Mrs. Saunders sat up straight in her chair and met him eye to eye.

"Mr. Blumberg, I don't know what grave predicaments you foresee for this boy, but I can assure you he's a good boy and a good student. And while I can certainly understand your concern about his falling asleep in class . . .''

"Twice, Mrs. Saunders. Twice." He held up two fingers to help out.

"Yes, twice. I can understand your concern about his falling asleep in class twice. And I do appreciate that in your line of work you've very likely heard every excuse in the book for every behavior imaginable. But I think you should know this. You see, in the past few years Tyler has had a number of allergic reactions. In fact, a few of his asthma attacks have been quite severe. To control these reactions, he sometimes needs strong medications, and these medications *can* cause drowsiness. And that is why sometimes, especially late in the afternoon, he's not at his best. His doctors are hopeful that he'll outgrow many of these allergies, and he'll no longer require medication. But he's a good boy, Mr. Blumberg. He really is. And I'm certain you'll find, medication or no medication, Tyler will turn out to be the kind of student Wakefield can be proud of." Mrs. Saunders spoke firmly and without hesitation. She had really done her homework. Perry Mason couldn't have defended me better.

"Mrs. Saunders, please understand," Mr. Blumberg said as nice as anybody could, "we wish the boy the best of luck with any medical problem he may be encountering. But, and forgive me for being blunt, I don't think all of Tyler's problems in school are by nature medical ones. We are, Mrs. Saunders, in the seventh day of school, and the boy has fallen asleep in class twice, he's been late once, without a legitimate excuse,

I might add, and he's been involved in two fights, one in school and one after school."

Mr. Blumberg sat back in his chair and studied Mrs. Saunders's reaction. I felt like I was watching a tennis match and it was Mrs. Saunders's serve.

"I'm afraid I'll have to take responsibility for his being late, Mr. Blumberg. And as for his fighting, well, I suppose I know as well as anyone that he can be a handful, a real handful . . . just like a lot of boys his age. But I think you'll find that given the chance, Tyler will settle into the routine soon enough."

"I don't think I need to remind you, Mrs. Saunders, that this is not the first school in which Tyler has experienced difficulties." He waved my permanent record folder and I squirmed in my seat. My head swiveled back to Mrs. Saunders. She still looked pretty strong.

"Mr. Blumberg, I think if you examine the whole record, you'll find that most of Tyler's school years have been flawless. His grades are fairly good, and most of his teachers have made a point of telling us he was a pleasure to have in class. He did have one bad semester, it's true, at a boarding school where he didn't belong in the first place. That was our mistake. A child belongs at home with the people who love him. But that's all in the past, and I don't think we'll see that kind of problem here." She met him head-to-head without flinching, even when she said "our mistake." Mrs. Saunders had been against that school from the start, but it wasn't like her to lay the blame on others.

"Mrs. Saunders," Mr. Blumberg said, nodding his head and looking as pleased as anything. "You bring up an excellent point. A child certainly does belong at home. But in addition to that, and forgive me for my

130

candor, I also feel very strongly that a child needs a full-time family.''

Mrs. Saunders stiffened at that and looked ready to jump down his throat. Mr. Blumberg smiled and held up his hand so he could continue.

''I'm simply trying to say that parenting is a full-time job. I know. I have a son myself. And it seems to me that a mother . . .'' He paused and seemed to grope with his hands for words. ''I'm sorry, but I must confess that I have difficulty with this modern notion of entrusting one's children to the care of others.''

I turned to see Mrs. Saunders's knuckles whiten as she gripped her purse. For a moment I thought she might clobber Mr. Blumberg with it.

''Mr. Blumberg, I'm afraid you don't quite understand our situation. You . . .''

''I may understand more than you realize. Correct me if I'm wrong. The boy's mother is out of the country. He is left to the care of a housekeeper, and . . .'' He threw his hands up in disbelief. ''And if no one else is available, he is watched by the groundskeeper. Now that's hardly the stability a child needs, wouldn't you agree, Mrs. Saunders?''

Suddenly I felt bewildered by the exchange. Mrs. Saunders had tears in her eyes, and it was plain to see that her hands were now shaking.

''That is terribly unfair, Mr. Blumberg. I am available as much as any real . . .''

Mr. Blumberg held up his hand again, smiling sadly now. He knew he was in control.

''Mrs. Saunders, I didn't mean for you to take personal offense. I'm certain you're doing an admirable job caring for the boy. I only have trouble with . . . how can I say it . . . the situation."

"The situation!" Mrs. Saunders had been about ready to burst into tears, but the way he said "situation" really rubbed her the wrong way. "You don't even begin to understand the situation." She was getting hot now, and patting my knee at the same time to show me that everything was all right. My jaw dropped down and my eyes popped wide. I could feel blood pulsing through the cuts and bruises on my face, and on top of that, I was starting to feel a little sick to my stomach like I do when I get tense.

"The situation is, Mrs. Saunders, that we see a child who needs, if anything, special care, being left behind by a woman who has obviously prioritized her career over her son!" He lost his smile, and for a second you could see something like anger or impatience flicker across his face.

Mrs. Saunders gasped. I felt like I'd been hit. My mouth was dry, and my tongue tried to stick to my teeth when I spoke.

"That's not true!" I yelled, tears starting. The blood seemed to drain from my head. I couldn't believe what I was hearing. He didn't even know my mother.

"Tyler, I'm sorry," said Mr. Blumberg, recovering quickly and smiling again. "I shouldn't have said that in front of you."

I glared at him, still shaking with anger. He didn't say he shouldn't have said it, only that he shouldn't have said it in front of me.

He turned to Mrs. Saunders.

"Perhaps we should have the boy wait outside."

"No!" I said before Mrs. Saunders had a chance to answer.

132

"Perhaps, honey, it would be best. I'll only be a minute." She spoke softly, but the way she looked at Mr. Blumberg, I knew she was bracing herself up for a real no-holds-barred battle.

"I'm not leaving," I said sullenly. That was the first time in my whole life that I could ever remember openly disobeying Mrs. Saunders. But it wouldn't be right to make her fight it out alone. It was my problem. Besides, there was no telling what kinds of things he might say if I wasn't there.

"I'll be all right," I said, still glaring at Mr. Blumberg, still smoldering inside.

"Perhaps," Mr. Blumberg continued calmly, "I'm wording this poorly. I didn't mean to be critical of the boy's mother. In fact, my own wife, who's as fine a woman as there is, would be working today if I had given her the choice." He paused and shook his head, giving us time to appreciate the difficulty of his decision. "But I remained firm on this one issue, and I believe it has paid off. My wife has her clubs and committees to keep her busy, and I believe, I really do, that this is why my son's permanent record folder doesn't . . . uh, shall we say, contain any surprises." He held up my folder as a kind of contrast.

"You really think your son is perfect, don't you?" Knowing what I knew about Mark made it impossible for me to keep quiet. Mrs. Saunders tried to shush me.

"I think his record speaks for itself." Again, the little flicker of anger across his face.

"Maybe the record should show that your son threw BooBoo Anderson in the quarry." My voice was quiet and cold. I felt like I was listening to someone else

133

speak. I heard Mrs. Saunders gasp, and I was afraid she might have her heart attack right then and there.

"Tyler!" Mrs. Saunders looked at me like I was a ghost. "This isn't doing any good!" Then turning. "Mr. Blumberg, this child's mother loves him as dearly as any mother could, and you've absolutely no right to imply otherwise. Look what you've done to him. He . . ."

"No, it's true," I yelled, knowing I had already gone past the point of no return. "You gotta pool, right? Yeah, you must have 'cause BooBoo was in your pool when he died. That's why he had chlorine in him!" I pointed an accusing finger. "They moved him . . . He was in your car!"

"Tyler, please!"

"It's true, Mrs. Saunders. I know it sounds crazy . . . they're hiding it . . . I saw it . . . I heard them . . ."

"Tyler!"

"Remember how he had chlorine in him! From their pool!"

"My dear boy," Mr. Blumberg said, remaining cool through all the yelling, smiling sadly like he was on to my childish game, but still had all the patience and understanding in the world. "This outburst merely substantiates my point. And not that I feel the need to respond to your wild accusation but for your own information, Bobby Anderson couldn't have drowned in my pool. On the night of that unfortunate incident I was home, in my own backyard, and next to the pool." He eyed me smugly, with a trace of pity that I would stoop so low.

"You'd lie to protect him, wouldn't you? You'd lie in a minute!"

"I'd much rather discuss your problems, which is

why we're here. But if you choose to further embarrass yourself, feel free to go out right now—I'll even give you a pass—to share this outlandish story with any teacher whom you feel you can trust.'' He reached into his desk and pulled out a book of blue passes. ''You see, on Saturday, almost all the teachers were in my backyard from early evening on. And a few of the hardier members of our staff were still there until after the drowning was reported. It was the night of our annual faculty party.''

''Then it happened in his friend Jack's pool!'' That had to be it.

''I'm afraid Jack's family doesn't have a pool.''

I turned to Mrs. Saunders. She was studying me sadly as if it was useless for her to say anything more until my tantrum had run its course. And from her too, I saw pity.

''I don't lie, Mrs. Saunders,'' I said, jumping up, tears streaming down my face. ''I don't lie . . . you know that . . . and I'm not crazy . . . I heard them . . . That's why I had to go out last night . . .'' I stopped, suddenly remembering that I had told her I left because I needed help in math. She stood with tears in her eyes and smoothed my hair back. She knew I was lying and felt sorry for me.

I couldn't look at her. And I couldn't look at Blumberg gloating from behind his big desk. I kicked at my chair like some kind of baby and darted into the hallway. Two secretaries stopped what they were doing at the office counter, their eyes fixed on me in wonder. I flew past them and kept running until I was a long way from school, and all those prying eyes. I didn't want to see anybody ever again.

# XV

I WISHED I had worn a jacket to school. Or at least a sweater. The sun was low and didn't have much heat left in it, and a steady breeze whipped across the water, chilling my bones with its dampness. I hadn't noticed it getting colder when I was walking, but I couldn't keep that up forever. I was about walked out. I had hiked to Lymie's place way out in the country the hard way, through the woods, across fields and meadows, climbing old rock fences and rusty barbed wire. It had taken me hours to get there. As it turned out, I'd even walked a few miles too far because I was quite a ways from the road and had lost track of where I was.

I had hidden like a convict in a tree overlooking Lymie's farm, far enough away so the dog wouldn't start yapping, hoping to see Lymie come out of the house or the barn alone. I spotted him once carrying a bale of hay out for the calves (I remembered how Lymie always cracked on me when I called them baby cows) in the pen next to the barn. I was about to hop down and sneak up on him when his father came out with another bale. I watched, sad and alone, as they fed the calves and got involved in some big conversation on their way to the house. Lymie's two little brothers came flying around the corner and zoomed into the house ahead of them. Dinner time. I could picture them all sitting around the big old table passing all kinds of food around. I was so hungry by this time I was tempted to run down and join them. But I knew that after I ate, Lymie's father would drive me home and I'd have to face the music.

Besides, I didn't really want to see anybody anyway. Not even Lymie. Come to think of it, after Lymie found out I'd blabbed the whole idiotic story about BooBoo a second time, I didn't suppose he'd want to see me either.

So I tramped back to the one place I knew of to hide out. A place where I could be alone and think.

The rock ledge I was dangling my legs over suddenly began to feel icy cold through my pants, and I stood up. I fired some flat shale rocks across the gray water and watched them skip and hop before losing momentum and sinking to the bottom. The last rock skipped five times before snagging the water and sinking in the exact spot that I'd swum into BooBoo. It seemed impossible that could have been just five days ago.

My stomach gnawed at me and my joints felt stiff and damp. I wanted more than anything to go home to my warm house, but I couldn't make myself do it. Maybe tomorrow. I couldn't face Mrs. Saunders tonight. My face still flushed when I thought about what I had said, and how I had slammed my way out of the office like a three-year-old having a tantrum. Maybe by tomorrow it wouldn't seem so bad. But I doubted that. This seemed like the type of rotten feeling that would linger for years.

I grabbed a sharp rock and began clearing a little cave

in the nearby brush that I could crawl into and get at least a little shelter. It wouldn't do much to keep out the cold, but at least working at it warmed me up some. After I'd hollowed out a narrow hole barely wide enough for me to squeeze into, I lay on my stomach and started sliding my legs in.

I lurched back and yelped. My nose was smack dab over a big pair of brown work shoes. I craned my head back and followed the work shoes up past a pair of jeans until I saw Chuckie's face staring down at me. His face was blank and he didn't say anything right away. I lowered my head back down between the shoes, waiting. I don't know what I was waiting for, but I knew better than to make a break for it. Chuckie was quick and athletic, and he'd snatch me back before I took two steps.

Something soft fell over my head blocking out the light.

"Put it on." It was one of my sweaters. I sat up and pulled it over my head. As soon as I was done, something else fell on me. My black denim jacket.

"Now put that on." Something in Chuckie's voice seemed to say I'd better do as I was told. Besides, I was still pretty cold. I buttoned my jacket and sat huddled up in a ball, trying to save what little body heat I had inside. Chuckie crouched down beside me, but he didn't say anything.

"How'd you find me?" I still wouldn't look at him.

"I went out to see your friend Lymie. He said you might be here."

"You heard what I did today?"

"I heard."

I waited to see if he had anything more to say. He didn't.

"So I guess you think I'm a liar along with everybody else."

"Did I say that?"

"You don't need to. I know what it looks like."

"Things don't always look like the way they are."

I peeked up. Chuckie was chewing on a blade of grass, not looking at me.

"Mrs. Saunders thinks I lied. I could tell."

"She didn't say that."

"She wouldn't. But I told her two different stories about why I went out last night. She knows one of them is a lie."

Chuckie stood up and grabbed me by the jacket.

"Let's go."

"I don't want to," I said sullenly.

"I want you to." He pulled me to my feet and waited while I brushed myself off. "So you're telling off principals now?"

"Blumberg's a big jerk. He thinks I'm no good because nobody cares about me." I walked to the rock ledge and stared across the water.

"Blumberg's not as bad as he seems. He's got his own problems."

"Yeah, like me," I said. "But he doesn't need to worry about that anymore. I'm not going back to that school."

"You're kind of conceited, aren't you?"

"No." That was about the only thing I wasn't.

"It seems to me you think everybody's problems revolve around you. I call that conceited."

"Yeah, and who made you a psychiatrist?"

"If I were a psychiatrist, I'd be charging you. I'm telling you this for free."

"Yeah, well, maybe you don't know as much as you think you do."

Chuckie pulled up alongside me, looking around like a tourist taking in the sights.

"I used to come here when I was a kid and wanted to be alone."

"Good try, Chuckie. Trying to make me feel like you were just like me. But I'm not buying it." I sat on the cold rocks. Chuckie did too.

"You know, it's funny," he said. "You tell me how Blumberg's a jerk, and yet you believe everything he says. But I can't get you to believe a word I say."

"Who said I believed him? I hate him."

Chuckie chewed on some more grass and thought for a minute.

"You might hate him. I don't know. You hated what he said, that's for sure. And I think it's because part of you really believes he was telling the truth."

"That's a load of bull. I can tell you that right now." I hate it when people think they know everything. Especially when they don't.

"Have it your way. You fly off the handle when some guy implies that your mother doesn't care about you, that she has to pay people to take care of you. And then you run off and hide because you don't think people care enough about you to trust you. What's it look like to you?"

"I took off because I made a fool of myself. Nobody likes to look like a total jerk."

"Oh, I see," Chuckie said quietly. "You're the jerk. I thought you said Blumberg was."

"If you're trying to make me look stupid, don't bother. You don't need to."

"Let me see if I understand this. You're stupid . . . and you're a liar . . . and you're a jerk. Whew! No wonder you thought Blumberg was telling the truth! But even if you were all those things, who ever told you a kid has to be perfect for people to care about him?"

"Perfect!" I yelled. "Everybody keeps saying that. You really think I want to be perfect? I'm a walking disaster area. Mom could retire on the money she's spent on my doctors. And you don't even know what happened at Grant Academy. You think the only stupid thing I ever did was piss my pants. Or tell off a principal. You don't know anything! You think you're so smart! You don't even know that I'm the one . . ." By now I was crying like crazy. Me, the kid that used to hardly ever cry at all.

Chuckie put a hand on my shoulder and spoke softly.

"I don't know that you're the one what?"

I drew in a heavy breath and turned away.

"I'm the one that drove my father out of the house! And even when he came back on Sundays, Mom and him still fought about me. You don't know anything!" I pulled away from Chuckie's hand and stood up. If I could have jumped into the gray water and disappeared, I would have.

Chuckie's grip, like cold iron, pulled my arm.

"Come on. We're going home."

I pulled against him but only feebly. I didn't have the strength or the will to put up much of a fight. I stumbled along miserably, like a guy on a chain gang. After a while Chuckie let go of my arm. I still trudged beside him, not even trying to get away.

"You know, Tyler, I know more about you than you might think."

"Yeah, like what?" I was being a mean, spoiled brat, but I didn't care.

He walked on for a minute without speaking.

"You remember when your mother bought your place right after finishing her last film?"

"No, my memory's bad, too."

Chuckie ignored the sarcasm.

"It was last spring, a few months before you moved here. Your mother hired me to start getting the place fixed up. I was out of the service, I needed a job, and that seemed like as good a job as any. Your mother stayed on for a week so she could show me what she wanted done. But she did more than that. She pitched right in and worked alongside me for the whole week. That impressed me, knowing that she could afford to have everybody else do her work for her, and yet seeing her in old clothes, hammering and scraping and painting."

"That's the way she is." I still sounded sulky, but I'm always a sucker for a story. I wondered what he was leading up to.

"Anyway, I really started to admire her. We talked a lot, and it wasn't long before I realized that she was really some kind of lady—smart, lively, interesting. She was good to have around. About the only thing I found wrong with her was the way she went on about you and your brother— you know the way parents do about their kids and it drives everybody crazy. I'd try to change the subject, but when she got wound up, there was no stopping her."

"Well, what did she say?" I stopped and looked up at him. He had me now. I'm such a sucker.

"I learned more about you and your brother in that

week than I ever wanted to know. Especially about you, probably because Chris was already grown up and on his own, and you were the one who was going to be living here. Actually most of it was kind of sickening, you know, how smart you were, how sweet and loving you were, how cute your little nose was . . ." He poked his finger at the tip of my nose and laughed.

"Cut it out, Chuckie."

"Anyway, she got to telling me how she was worried that she and your father had made life so difficult for you. She said she really needed to make it up to you. All I could picture was this spoiled rich kid whose mother would be willing to give him the sun and the moon if he asked. I didn't like you and I hadn't even met you yet."

"Why did she think that she and Dad made life difficult for me? I'm the one who made things tough for them."

Chuckie looked back at the red sun which was dropping down fast and gave me a little push to get me moving again.

"Can't you walk and talk at the same time, Ace? She said how a little while before you were born, things had already gotten pretty bad between her and your father. In fact, your father moved out and took an apartment downtown. Your mother told me they had been married too young, and as they both got older and learned more about who they each were, trouble started that just wouldn't go away. They couldn't agree on anything. Your father thought your mother should give up her career, for one thing, to take care of your brother. But it wasn't only that. No matter what the subject was, if one of them thought one way, the other thought the opposite. But when they found out you were on the way, they decided to get back together and try one more time to make a go of it.''

"How come Mom told *you* all that stuff?" I asked him. "She never said anything to me."

"I don't know. But it was all leading up to you. She wanted me to know all about you. Maybe so I'd understand you better. I don't know. And your mother probably figured you were too young to know about that kind of trouble. Even your brother didn't know any of this at the time. He was only eight or nine then, and he thought your father had been away on a job.''

"So what'd she say about me?" I stopped and looked at him again.

"I'm getting to that, Ace." He gave me another little shove to get me going. "So they got back together and you were born, with your cute little nose, which personally I don't find all that irresistibly cute, and you were one big happy family again. At least that's what your mother wanted you and Chris to think. Actually your parents still couldn't agree on anything. And when you started having asthma attacks, and breaking out in hives, and all the other stuff you did, your parents thought it was psychosomatic, you know, all in your head. And both of them blamed the other for screwing you up. That's what your mother felt the worst about, looking back on it. You had become an excuse for them to fight. You were in the middle of a tug-of-war you didn't even know about. It finally got so bad they couldn't stay together, and they split up for good.''

We were on the street now, less than a block from my house. I stopped again.

"I used to hear them fighting about me all the time.

I thought that if I was a better kid . . . you know . . . if I was less trouble . . .''

"Ace, your parents couldn't even agree on your name, and they were fighting about that before you were even born. So how could it have possibly been something you did?" He walked on past me. "There was one thing they agreed on."

"What?" I said and caught up to him.

"As much as they fought, they did love you very much. Your father too."

It seemed funny hearing a tough guy like Chuckie using the word "love."

"Mom always told me how much Dad thought of me, but I figured she only said it to make me feel better."

"Well, she told it to me too, and that's the God's honest truth. And I don't think she was trying to make me feel better." He stopped next to the archway at the end of our driveway. "So don't get smart thinking you're hiding some deep, dark secret from me."

It was hard to believe. All these years I thought I was a major disappointment in my father's life, and that disappointment was the main thing that came between him and Mom. I guess people tried to set me straight before, but I never completely believed them. It turned out Chuckie knew more about me than I knew about myself.

"Chuckie, can we go to your place? I'm still not ready to face Mrs. Saunders after what I did today."

"Yeah, why not," Chuckie said, turning toward his cottage. "But I'll never understand how you're able to squeeze so much guilt into such a little body."

"I'm not that little," I said, following him. And I couldn't believe it. I felt better than I had in a long time.

# XVI

CHUCKIE MADE ME take a hot shower to get warmed up while he made something for us to eat. I knew he'd call Mrs. Saunders right away, but I didn't mind. I couldn't face her yet, but I didn't want her worrying herself sick over me either.

Chuckie was a lousy cook. He managed to burn the canned spaghetti to the bottom of the pan while the top of it was still cold. And then he scooped out some ice cream right into our dirty spaghetti dishes. It was just as well. I wasn't supposed to eat too much stuff like that anyway because sugar makes me hyper. Chuckie was funny to watch, like some clumsy mother hen, spilling things all over and yelling at me that I didn't eat enough. He cleared the dishes, dumped them into the already overflowing sink, and then sat looking at me.

"So what are you going to do now?" he asked me.

"About what?"

"You said you knew something about what happened to BooBoo. So what are you going to do about it?"

"Are you kidding me, Chuckie?" I said, irritated that he would bring that up when I was finally feeling good again. "There's nothing I can do. Nobody will believe me now." I sat for a minute, thinking. "I don't understand it. I must be going crazy or something. I sat right there and heard those guys talking about BooBoo. And since the police said he had chlorine in him, and his mother said he was going to Mark's place, I was sure that whatever happened happened at Blumberg's pool. But now . . . I don't know . . . I'm really confused."

"But you and Lymie did see a car that could have been Blumberg's at the rock quarry the night you found the body."

I looked up, surprised. Chuckie smiled when he saw the bug-eyed look on my face.

"Lymie told me all about it," he said. "I thought his mother was going to kill him. And I'm not sure Mrs. Saunders isn't going to kill you when she finds out."

"Wow, Lymie told you that even though he knew he'd get in trouble." I was beaming all over the place. Now at least Chuckie wouldn't think I was completely off my rocker.

"Let me see," Chuckie said, sitting back and rubbing his chin. "Blumberg said he was at his poolside with a group of teachers all night, right?"

"Yeah, that's what I don't get. They were there from early evening till way past midnight."

"That's strange. I remember seeing Blumberg's car in front of the school that night. I didn't think anything of it at the time. I figured Blumberg was catching up on some office work."

I popped up in my seat.

"So, Chuckie, Blumberg must be lying!"

"Not likely," Chuckie said. "He wouldn't be dumb enough to lie about that many witnesses having seen him."

"Then what?" I said, studying his face to see if he had anything.

"Think about it a minute, Ace. Blumberg is home and most of his teachers are with him. BooBoo is heading for his house, but supposedly never gets there. BooBoo dies in a pool, but it couldn't have been Blumberg's. And Blumberg's car is at the school."

"The pool in the school!" I shouted. "That's where they went. The school keys are probably right on Blumberg's key chain. That's gotta be where they went!"

"Maybe. It wouldn't surprise me a bit. But we don't have any proof."

"So what should we do? What do you think?"

"Well, we can't do anything about it tonight. And you've already had a busy enough day. You look kind of bleary-eyed. I say we'd better get you home to bed."

"Chuckie?"

"What?"

"Can I stay here tonight? I know I've already been a lot of trouble and I'm sorry, but, I don't know, I'm still not ready to go home."

Chuckie looked at me a minute before saying anything.

"I guess that would be all right. I only have a twin bed. You take it and I'll sleep on the couch."

"No, I've already been enough trouble. I'll grab some blankets and make a bed on the floor of your room." I was old enough not to be afraid to sleep in a room alone, but with all the thoughts racing through my head, I didn't want to take any chances with nightmares. I hoped Chuckie wouldn't figure that out.

"Suit yourself," Chuckie said, like it was no big

148

deal. "There are plenty of blankets in the hall closet. You take care of that, and I'll call Mrs. Saunders."

I headed for the blankets and stopped, thinking.

"Chuckie, can you, I don't know, can you tell Mrs. Saunders that I'm really sorry about this afternoon? I still can't believe I did that."

"Still giving yourself a hard time, huh, pal? Don't worry about it. I'll tell her. But you know, it gets pretty tiresome hearing you apologize for yourself. It's starting to get on my nerves."

"Sorry," I said and then laughed when I realized what I'd done.

"I expected you to say that," Chuckie said, "so why am I so surprised?" He looked at me like I had two heads, then shook his head and threw up his arms. He was still mumbling something I couldn't quite make out as he left. I started grabbing all the blankets I could get my hands on. One thing about me, I can never get too warm.

Chuckie's bedroom looked a little like mine would have looked if Mrs. Saunders didn't help me keep it cleaned up. I cleared off a spot right next to the bed and folded a couple blankets in half, laying them out on the carpeting. I threw the rest on top. Then I hopped out of my clothes, burrowed into my homemade bed, and closed my eyes. It had been a full day and I was pretty beat. I could hear Chuckie in the other room on the phone, but I couldn't tell what he was saying. I wished I could come up with a brilliant plan to snag Mark and Jack before I went to sleep, but my mind was too fuzzy to think straight.

A moment later a pillow whacked me over the head.

"I thought you might want this. Don't apologize again. It's an extra one."

Chuckie snapped off the light and turned to leave the room.

"Chuckie?"

"What do you need now, Ace?"

"Remember when you were talking about Blumberg?" I propped myself up on my elbows. "What did you mean when you said he had problems of his own?"

"It's a long story, Ace, but I'll see if I can keep it short." He sat on the edge of his bed. "You see, Blumberg's wife used to be an actress in New York, a pretty good one from what I've heard. When they first moved upstate, his wife was in an off-Broadway play, and she was away most of the time. Rumor had it that when Mark arrived, Blumberg forbid her to work until he was grown up. Well, she went along with him, but people who know them say she's never been the same. She goes through the motions of being his wife, but it's like she's never really forgiven him. Like he took something that wasn't his to take."

"Wow," I said, thinking. "Maybe that's why Mark turned out so mean. You know, growing up with all that resentment around him."

"I wouldn't be surprised."

"I bet everybody'd have been better off in the end if she went ahead and did what she wanted like my mom did."

"That wouldn't surprise me either. But anyway, the point is that when your mother moved here with you, and the whole town was buzzing about having a famous actress around, well, it was tough on both of them. People say she won't even look at him anymore."

"And that's why Blumberg wanted to prove to everybody that I turned out so lousy, I bet. Maybe so everybody would think he was right.''

"Maybe. Or maybe he just wanted to believe it himself. I don't know. But it's harder to hate a guy when you see that he's got problems like everybody else.''

"I don't hate him any more," I said. I felt kind of sorry for him. And her, too.

"Yeah, I know," Chuckie said, standing up and walking to the lighted doorway. "Now get some sleep.''

"Chuckie?''

He stopped, silhouetted in the doorway.

"I almost made it that time. What now, Ace?''

"Remember how you said you didn't like me even before you met me? Did you . . . you know . . . have you changed your mind about me at all?''

"I'm crazy about you, Ace. I don't know how I managed to live all these years without you. There is one thing though." He paused for a second. "Try not to piss all over my floor.''

I felt my cheeks get hot. I could see Chuckie's outline in the doorway, his head cocked sideways. I knew he was wearing a big stupid smile and waiting to see if I'd go hyper or throw something at him.

"Sure, Chuckie, as long as you promise not to throw up all over me.''

At that he burst out laughing. I did, too.

"You're learning. It's a deal. Now no more dumb questions. We'll talk tomorrow.''

I had to admit I felt like a pretty lucky kid. In a new town I hadn't even wanted to come to, I already had three of the best friends anybody could want: Lymie, Mary Grace, and Chuckie.

Not bad for a lemon.

# XVII

CHUCKIE WOKE ME early the next morning. I half remember snuggling my head into my pillow and mumbling for him to leave me alone. Chuckie grabbed the blankets I was sleeping on and gave them a good yank, spinning me across the floor like a tipped-over top.

"What are you, crazy?"

"Maybe a little. But I'm sane enough to see that you get to school." He was snatching up the blankets quicker than I could wrap myself back into them.

"You are crazy!" I said, gawking up at him like he was some kind of madman. "I can't go to school today."

"You look healthy enough to me."

"For all I know I'm expelled or something. Come on, Chuckie, be serious. You know I can't go back there."

"You can't?" Chuckie gasped, wrapping his hands around his jaws and pretending to be surprised. "Oh, my goodness gracious, I forgot. Quick, we've got to find a cave to hide you in. At least till Blumberg dies of old age. Or maybe after twenty years the President will pardon you, and you can once again be with us who believe in you, a free man at last.'' Chuckie jerked me to my feet and clasped me in his arms. ''Just remember, we'll think of you every day.''

''That's really funny, Chuckie,'' I said, shaking myself loose. ''But I'm not going.''

''Oh, yes,'' he said. ''You're going all right. Now quit wasting time. You get ready for school and I'll cook breakfast.'' He shoved some fresh school clothes in my gut and shoved me toward the bathroom. He must have gone over to my house earlier to get them. I got the feeling from the look on his face that even if I dropped dead, he'd still drag me to school. And on time.

Maybe it wouldn't be so bad. Maybe nobody'd even heard what I did yesterday. After all, it wouldn't be too smart for Blumberg to broadcast the whole thing. Even if he did figure Mark had an airtight alibi, there were enough people around who would be only too glad to believe Mark would be involved in something rotten. And deep down inside, Blumberg probably knew this. It might not be so awful. Unless I got in trouble I probably wouldn't even see Blumberg all day.

Besides, I didn't have any choice.

At breakfast I asked Chuckie if he had come up with any ideas. He shook his head.

''Nothing specific. But I know that if you have no evidence and no witnesses, you'll have to hope one of the guys confesses. There's no other way.''

''Fat chance of that,'' I mumbled disappointedly.

''Don't be too sure. Haven't you ever read *Macbeth*?''

''No, I read *Romeo and Juliet*, but I don't think that applies here.''

"You surprise me, Ace. I thought you were an expert on guilt."

"Only my own," I said.

"Yeah, well we're working on that, aren't we? Let's see. How about the 'The Telltale Heart' by Edgar Allan Poe? You must have read that."

"Yeah, I read that," I told him. I even liked it. It was about this crazy guy who killed an old man just because he didn't like the way he looked. Only he didn't know what to do with the body, so he chopped it up in little pieces which he buried under the floorboards. I figured that's how he'd get caught, when it started to smell, but it never got a chance to. When the police come to question him, he starts hearing the old guy's heart beating under the floorboards, even though the guy is dead and all chopped up. Of course the police don't hear a thing. They're still as friendly as can be. But finally the heartbeat gets so loud to the crazy guy that he jumps up and confesses the whole thing. I couldn't believe it.

"That's a good story, Chuckie, but what do you want me to do, follow Mark and Jack around making heartbeat noises?"

Chuckie ignored the wisecrack and leaned forward, thinking.

"Listen, Ace, if somebody has a guilty conscience about something, it's like that guilt is crying out inside them all the time. Except they're the only ones who can hear it. But if it's loud enough inside them, they start thinking other people can hear it too. Or see it in their faces. And if the guilt gets bad enough, they just might confess to save themselves the mental agony."

"I think Mark's conscience is on permanent hold. He probably wouldn't confess even if we had pictures."

"Maybe. But what about the other guy? All it takes is for one of them to break."

"Yeah, that's right," I said, getting excited again. "Jack was really bugged about the whole thing. He was all worried that the police didn't believe them, and he even said he hadn't been able to sleep right since that night."

"Well, that's a good sign. And that was even before he knew anybody was on to him."

"So we should probably do something to make him talk, huh? What do you think, Chuckie?"

"Slow it down, Ace. Don't go rushing into anything. It might be that he's shaken enough right now so he's ready to confess on his own. If not, then we'll try to think of something. But I don't want to see you going off half-cocked and getting into more trouble. Take your time and see what happens."

That's a thing that always happens to people when they get older. They always figure everything can keep. Me, I couldn't wait to try something.

"I'll see if Mary Grace and Lymie have any ideas."

"You do that, Ace. And let me know if you come up with anything." Then he grabbed me by the shirt and pulled my face up to his. "But listen and listen good," he said. "Don't do anything stupid. If Jack and Mark have something to hide and they're scared, I don't trust them."

"All right, all right. Don't get all bent out of shape. I can take care of myself."

"Right," he said, letting me go and handing me my bookbag. But he didn't look too convinced.

# XVIII

MARK AND JACK leaned against the wall, cool and tough, their thumbs hitched into their jeans pockets, watching everybody go by. I thought about making a U-turn and almost did. Then Jack spotted me and elbowed Mark. They both straightened up and glared at me without blinking.

I did something then that surprised even me. I walked right toward them and smiled. Not a big flashy smile like a car salesman would give you, just a little "isn't it good to be alive" smile. I stared at them, still smiling, as I walked past. Mark clenched his teeth and mumbled something to Jack. Jack still looked mean, but his eyes were on his shoes now. When I got a ways down the hall, I shot another happy face their way. For a second, I thought Mark would come after me, but he didn't. And Jack looked downright sickly.

Chuckie was right.

I hurried to study hall. Lymie, Mary Grace, and I all had library passes, and I couldn't wait to sign out. Both of them had been after me since before homeroom to tell them what the big deal was, but I wouldn't say a word, only that they should meet me in the library third period.

The library was pretty empty when the three of us arrived. We plopped our passes on the librarian's desk. She kind of gave us the evil eye, probably because we walked in together. I told her I was looking for *Macbeth* because I needed to grab *something*, and she wrinkled up her face and pointed to the card catalog. Things like that always kill me. It was a small library and she probably knew where every book in the place was by heart, but all she could do was point at the card catalog. Lymie headed for the magazine rack and grabbed a *Hot Rodder* magazine, and Mary Grace browsed through fiction.

We met at a table in the back corner like we had agreed on and tried to look busy. If we seemed to be in the mood for conversation, we'd be split up right away. We waited a few minutes for the librarian to stop gawking at us and get back to her own work. Pretty soon another suspicious-looking group arrived, and she started eyeing them.

I leaned forward and pretended to be sharing a passage from *Macbeth* with Lymie. Lymie looked funny peeking out from behind his *Hot Rodder* magazine, pretending to be interested in *Macbeth*. Mary Grace kept her eyes in her own book.

"I told Blumberg about Mark and Jack," I mumbled, pointing to a Lady Macbeth speech.

"I don't believe it!" Lymie said. "Is there anybody you haven't told?"

I glared at him and he fixed his eyes back on the speech.

"Let him tell the story." Mary Grace's voice floated out from a mouth that didn't move.

157

"I couldn't help it, Lymie. Blumberg got nasty about my mother, and I got all hyper. It was pretty bad. I yelled at him and everything. He thinks I'm a mental case now for sure."

"Wow," Lymie said quietly, as if he were in the presence of greatness. "No wonder you ran away!"

"Tyler, you ran away?"

"Yeah, he did. Chuckie, this guy who works for him, came around looking for him. I tell you, I wouldn't want that guy mad at me."

"Tyler, why did you run away?" Mary Grace asked.

"You should see the arms on that guy," Lymie said.

I rolled my eyes. "Does anybody want to hear what I have to say? I thought that's why we were here."

"All right, all right. Shut up and tell us!" Lymie's voice carried across the library. The way the librarian flinched, you'd think something had hit her in the head. We buried our faces in our books and magazines, not saying anything for quite a while. Finally she started shelving books.

"Now listen," I said through my teeth. "Don't say anything. Just listen." I felt like a ventriloquist whose dummy had been stolen.

I probably looked pretty foolish, but I did manage to get the whole story out without us being split up. I had to kick Lymie in the shins a few times to shut him up, and he did threaten to kill me once, but at least I got it out. The whole time Mary Grace's eyes were glued to her book, and a couple of times I could've sworn she was reading it.

"Well anyway, that's what Chuckie said." I took a deep breath and looked at both of them.

Lymie shook his head. I should have known he'd

158

never come up with a plan because he never thinks anything will work. And Mary Grace looked like she wanted to finish her book. What a pair!

"Is the book really that good?" I said. "I mean it's only BooBoo's murder we're talking about here."

"I think Chuckie is right." Her voice floated out of her mouth again. "Jack is the one to work on. Even when Mark was a little kid, he'd never admit anything even if ten people saw him do it. But Jack, he's another story. He's scared already."

"You've got an idea?" I should have apologized for making that sarcastic remark about her book, but before I could, she had already launched herself into the details of her plan. And a beautiful plan it was—a cat and mouse plan where we got to be the cats. Even Lymie looked thrilled, and that's saying something.

"Do either of you have any plain white paper?" Mary Grace asked.

I had a bunch left over from my stupid science project which I was falling further behind on every day. I was glad to find a good use for it since I still hadn't collected any decent rocks, and I'd rather hand in nothing than those painted crushed stones.

Lymie and I watched, amazed, as Mary Grace took out a red magic marker and started drawing up a sign in her perfect block letter printing. I tingled with excitement as she finished the first one.

"Okay, Tyler, put this one up on the gym bulletin board outside Mr. Johnson's office. Try not to be seen." She started in on the next one. "And Lymie, you put this one in the main foyer, and I'll put one up on the cafeteria bulletin board."

"Mary Grace," I said, hoping I didn't sound too

much like Lymie always did, "how do we keep the teachers or Blumberg from seeing these signs and yanking them down?"

"That shouldn't be a problem. For one thing, I don't think Mr. Johnson ever looks at his own bulletin board. If the janitors didn't keep the graffiti off it, the gym probably would've been raided by the police by now. As for the other two, by the time a teacher or somebody finds them, who knows how many kids will have seen them already."

"It'll work, Tyler," Lymie said gruffly. "Don't be such a worrywart."

I bit my lip and let that one slide.

After Mary Grace finished the last sign, we all sat restless and fidgety waiting for the bell. When it rang I flew for the door like a shot and got yelled at for not signing out my book. I raced back to the desk.

"Sorry, I forgot."

"I'll bet you did," she said, giving me the evil eye again. Like I came to school just to steal her book.

I snatched the book off her desk almost before she lifted her stamp and zoomed toward the gym. A steady stream of kids filed into the boys' locker room. I hung around the bulletin board pretending to read announcements until the coast was clear. Then I grabbed a spare tack out of the football schedule and stuck up our phony sign.

I stepped back for a second to admire it.

DUE TO THE SUCCESS OF LAST SATURDAY'S
SMALL PARTY AT THE SCHOOL POOL
ANOTHER PARTY WILL BE HELD THIS SAT.
AT 8:00 P.M.

SIGN UP LIMITED TO FIRST ONE HUNDRED
SO DON'T WAIT
SEE JACK ROBBINS TO SIGN UP
BEFORE 3:00 TODAY

Beautiful.

# XIX

I'M NOT MUCH in the patience department. A whole period passed and nobody even mentioned the pool party. I was going crazy. Maybe Mrs. Saunders was right. She always said people don't read any more. Mary Grace told me to relax.

At lunchtime the sign in the cafeteria started to draw some attention. A bunch of kids clustered around the bulletin board chattering away and pointing, and that's all it took. Nothing draws a crowd like a crowd. Pretty soon big kids were pushing their way through, and little kids were craning their necks to see what the excitement was. Mary Grace poked me and told me to act natural and quit staring. I tried, but every few minutes my head would swivel back to the action like a compass needle. Not that it mattered much. A lot of other kids were staring too.

On the way out I passed by the announcement and sneaked a peek. A strand of spaghetti was hanging from it and there was some chocolate milk or something splattered on it, and somebody had written EAT ME on the bottom, but it was still pretty readable considering.

Posters and cafeterias both bring out the animal in kids. Put the two together and you're asking for trouble.

Before social studies class everybody was talking about signing up for the party. A few kids had already tried and said Jack had been pretty nasty to them. Nobody thought that was too strange. Eighth graders are used to being shafted by older kids. Everybody figured Jack wanted to save room for all his high school buddies. A few of the activist types said it was unfair and they started up a petition saying that if the junior high kids weren't allowed to sign up, we should be able to have a party on our own. At the last minute they changed the junior high part to eighth graders because they didn't want to hang around with little seventh grade kids.

I even signed it. What the heck.

After fifth period I ran across Jack in the hall. He was swamped by kids trying to make sure they got signed up. As he pushed his way through the crowd, kids kept jumping in front of him trying to stop him. His face was bright red, and he looked like he was about ready to cry. I stood there and watched for a minute before going to class. I could hardly believe it, but I was starting to feel sorry for him. And guilty about what we were doing. Chuckie was right. I really had to work on that.

Turning to go to class, I drove my nose into some big kid's chest. When I looked up, I found myself staring at Mark Blumberg. He didn't say a word, but his jaw was clenched and his eyes were meaner than I'd ever seen them. I swallowed hard and stood frozen in my tracks until he shoved me out of his way with his forearm, hard enough so my books went flying. I hoped

Mary Grace was right about him. But he sure did look like he could be a killer.

During sixth period, Jack was called to the office over the P.A. Mary Grace poked me in the back. Ten minutes later I was called to the office. I sat for a minute feeling the blood drain from my head. Mary Grace jabbed me.

"Remember," she whispered, "you didn't write those announcements."

As I walked out of the room she smiled and gave me the thumbs up. I tried to smile back. My heart was beating something fierce.

They were waiting for me in the office. Mr. Blumberg motioned impatiently for me to take a seat. Jack was already in a chair, and he looked pretty shaken. He didn't look mean now, just plain scared.

"Mr. McAllister," Mr. Blumberg began, "it seems that hardly a day goes by that I don't find it necessary to have a little chat with you. I have a few questions I'd like to ask, and if you would be so kind, I'd appreciate some honest answers."

I nodded.

"Mr. McAllister, have you seen the announcements concerning tomorrow's supposed pool party?" He held up two of Mary Grace's signs and waved them in front of me. One of them still said EAT ME. Probably the one in the gym was still up.

I nodded again.

"Mr. Robbins seems to think, and I suspect with good reason, that you are responsible for these. I'd like to hear what you have to say about this." He leaned forward and studied my face.

I gulped. Then I shrugged.

"Did you write these?" Mr. Blumberg snapped, his voice jumping up a few notches. "I'd like a simple yes or no."

"No." I looked down.

"You swear you're not responsible for these? Look at me, please."

I looked.

"I'm not. I swear." As long as he asked the question that way, I was safe.

Mr. Blumberg looked tired. He rubbed his eyes, shook his head, and threw up his hands.

"Mr. Robbins, could you give us, perhaps, at least an inkling as to why you think Mr. McAllister wrote these?" He sat back and waited. So did I.

"I don't know, but I know he did it. He hates me. He probably figured he could get me in trouble." He gave me a sullen look.

Jack sounded so scared I was starting to feel sorry for him all over again. And that's saying something, because I was pretty busy being scared myself.

"Perhaps you could explain, Mr. Robbins, why you feel Mr. McAllister hates you so much he is bent on revenge?"

"I don't know," Jack said, squirming in his seat. "He just does."

Mr. Blumberg closed his eyes and pinched the bridge of his nose. When he opened them, they were fixed on me.

"Do you hate Mr. Robbins?"

"No, not really."

"Then, Mr. McAllister, let me rephrase the question. Do you like him?"

I looked at Jack and Jack looked at me.

"I don't know. I don't really know him that well."

Mr. Blumberg closed his eyes again and took in a couple of deep breaths. I was afraid he might be getting ready to have some kind of attack. When he finally spoke, I could barely hear him.

"Both of you may return to class until I decide what to do about this."

I was surprised he didn't tell us not to leave town. I dashed out the door and hustled back to class so that I wouldn't have to face Jack alone in the hall. No sooner had I slid into my seat than Mr. Blumberg's voice sounded over the P.A. announcing there would be no pool party.

One of the kids with the petition looked up and said, "I wonder if this means we can't have ours either?"

# XX

I HEARD THE lawn mower buzzing around the backyard. Tossing my bookbag onto the porch, I ran out
to find Chuckie, anxious to fill him in on what we'd
done to Jack. Chuckie turned off the little John Deere
tractor and listened as I rambled excitedly through all
the details. He didn't say a word.

"Well?" I said. "I bet that'll make him confess.
You think?"

"I don't know, Ace. I thought we were going to hold
off for a while."

"Hold off for what, Chuckie? We had a good plan.
Why should we wait?" Chuckie wasn't the type to get
all excited and hop around like a kid, but I had expected
more enthusiasm than this.

"You have to be careful about pushing people too
hard into corners. You could get hurt."

"Aw, come on, Chuckie. You don't really think those
guys are dangerous, do you?" I thought about how I'd
smiled and stared them down earlier.

"Anybody can be dangerous if they're pushed hard
enough. So don't get too impatient."

"Yeah, right," I said, not even trying to hide how

annoyed I was. I figured he was probably mad that he didn't think up his own plan.

He put his hand on my shoulder and shook his head slowly.

"Ace, I'm not putting the plan down. All I'm saying is be careful. I don't want to see you get beat up again."

"I can take care of myself," I said sullenly. "Don't worry about it."

"Yeah, you're right. I'm sorry," he said, punching my arm. And then, "Oh, by the way, Ace, are your other pants dry yet?"

He blocked my swing before it connected with his jaw and wrestled me to the ground before I had a chance to swing again. And all the while he was laughing like some kind of a nut. I squirmed and kicked and swore, but Chuckie was about ten times stronger than me, and I ended up with nothing for my trouble but a mouthful of grass.

"Sorry to get you riled, Ace," Chuckie said, after his laughing fit had passed, "but I've never known anybody who could completely take care of himself, let alone a twelve-year-old with a bad temper."

"I'll kill you, Chuckie!" I spit out some grass.

"I'm waiting, Ace," Chuckie said. "Make your move."

I flailed around a little more and then let myself go limp under his weight. It was no use.

"Why do you have to keep bringing up about me pissing my pants when you know it bothers me? Is that how you get your kicks?" I spit out some more grass.

"When it stops bothering you, then I won't have any reason to bring it up, will I?"

"You're probably going to tell everybody. That is, if you haven't already."

"I told you I wouldn't. I don't go back on my word." He stood up. I rolled over and looked up at him.

"Yeah, you told me. But sometimes . . ."

"Sometimes what, Ace?"

"I don't know. Sometimes I think you deliberately try to get me mad."

"Oh, I do," Chuckie said smiling. "Definitely I do."

"Why?" I said, sitting up.

"Because you're too sensitive for your own good, Ace. That makes you a hothead, a reactor."

"A reactor?" I understood the hothead part.

"Yeah, a reactor is somebody who reacts to everybody around him. They do something and he reacts—bing! He's letting other people call the shots. They control whether he's happy, sad, mad, or whatever. And if you're a hothead on top of that, then you're really at their mercy."

I thought about that for a minute.

"You mean like how I blew up at Blumberg?"

"Yeah, that's one example. If you know what your mother is like, it shouldn't matter what anybody else thinks. It has nothing to do with you. Or like now, when I cracked on you for pissing your pants. I was ready to block your punch before you even decided to swing. You were letting me control you."

"But Chuckie, if you never reacted to anybody, then you'd be like a zombie or something, you know, stumbling around in your own little world. Then people could do whatever they wanted to you."

"All I'm saying, Ace, is that you should stay in control and call the shots yourself. You should decide what

169

you want to do, what's best to do. Don't go flying off the handle without thinking.''

That made sense. I remembered how when I smiled at Mark and Jack that morning, I felt like I was in control, forcing them to react to me, like Chuckie said. That felt good for a change.

"Work on it, Ace. That's all. You're not going to change overnight, but keep trying."

"I will, Chuckie," I told him. "Yeah, I will."

Chuckie sat down next to me, and we stayed quiet for a while, staring out across the yard.

"Chuckie?"

"Yeah, Ace?"

"You think Mrs. Saunders will let me go to Buster's tonight?"

He laughed.

"Don't even ask. You don't have a chance. You better let things cool down for a few days before making plans to resume your social life.''

"Is she mad?"

"No, she's not mad. But I have a feeling she'll want to keep her eye on you for a while."

"She's afraid I'll screw up again?"

"No, she worries, that's all. She takes care of you. She's got a right to worry." He hopped to his feet.

"Chuckie?"

"Why do I get the feeling we're playing Twenty Questions?"

"Maybe you could ask her. You know, about me going to Buster's. Maybe you could even bring me there. Then she couldn't say no."

"Forget it, Ace. Stay home and out of trouble for a

change. Besides, I have to go to Albany to pick up something tonight.''

''Didn't you ever hear of UPS?''

''No,'' Chuckie said, like it was news to him. ''Did you ever hear of lawn mowing?'' He picked me up by the elbows and set me on the tractor seat. ''Finish up, will you, and I'll get my other work done.''

''No problem, Chuckie. This kid was made to mow.''

''Yeah, I bet. Just make sure you don't drive through the side of the house or something.'' He started to walk away. ''Hey, Ace?''

''What?'' I said, reaching down for the key.

''See that the seat stays dry, huh?''

That cracked him up. He was still laughing as he disappeared around the corner. I had to laugh too when I thought about it.

I finished the lawn without doing anything stupid like wracking up or chopping anything that shouldn't have been chopped, things I'd been known to do in the past.

And I was still laughing whenever I thought about Chuckie and his stupid wet pants jokes. And I started thinking, maybe there's still hope for me.

# XXI

I KNOW MRS. Saunders doesn't mean any harm, but when you're going on thirteen, a little hugging and kissing goes a long way. The way she carried on you'd think I'd been away for twenty years. My mom's the same way. When they're both around, they're on me like fly paper.

And I was glad Chuckie wasn't around to hear all the apologizing I did. The whole scene would have made him throw up worse than he did in the driver ed. room that time. But it felt good to have things back to normal between me and Mrs. Saunders, to know she'd still be there for me no matter what stupid stunt I might pull next. Good thing, too—I was already planning what she might consider my next stupid move.

I had to get out of the house and go to Buster's to see if our plan had driven Jack to confess yet. If he'd done it, somebody at Buster's would know about it. Chuckie had already told me not to even bother asking for permission, so I wasn't going to. I told Mrs. Saunders that I was pretty beat and I was going to bed early. I knew that would make her happy, knowing how she feels about sleep. I even got undressed and climbed into

172

bed so I wouldn't feel like such a liar. But by 8:30 I was out the window and shimmying down one of the porch columns. Chuckie had already left by then, so it was no sweat about getting caught. And it's only about ten times faster to escape when you're not dragging Lymie behind you.

Buster's was already alive with its usual grubby Friday night crowd when I arrived. There was a greasy thickness of cigarette smoke and fumes from the grill that made voices and the electronic bleeps and bloops of the video games seem to hang suspended in midair. Kids milled around in bunches, talking loudly, eyeing what little action there was restlessly, impatiently, waiting, like they were expecting something more. The weekend everybody had lived all week for had arrived, and no one seemed to know what to do with it.

I slipped silently through the crowd looking for Lymie. He said he'd try to get a ride to town if he could talk his mother out of grounding him for sneaking out with me to the quarry. Which was somewhere between highly unlikely and never in a million years. So it didn't surprise me that I couldn't find him. And I knew I wouldn't see Mary Grace. Kids like her didn't go to Buster's. I stuck a token into the only game that wasn't being played and started bombing terrorists and saving hostages with this helicopter. Except the game was set up too close to one of the pool tables, and high school kids kept shoving me out of their way or jabbing their cue sticks into my ribs, and I ended up annihilating about fifty hostages. Lymie didn't know it, but he wasn't missing much. Mary Grace probably did know it, and that's why she wasn't there.

I gave up on the game before it was finished and

173

snaked my way around trying to find a corner with some space I could call my own. I made it to the back, half under my own power and half under the power of the big kids I bumped up against.

I saw Jack standing alone behind the last pool table. He looked sickly and miserable. He spotted me, and I froze in my tracks. Next thing I knew he was headed my way, and I tried to scoot out through the crowd. Before I'd gone two steps, I bashed into this fat kid who looked like he wanted to body slam me or something. As I backed out of his range, somebody grabbed my arm.

"We have to talk." It was Jack. He didn't say it mean. His voice was dull and tired. But he didn't let go of my arm.

"Okay, so talk."

"Not here. Outside." He jerked his thumb toward the rear exit.

"Where's Mark?" I asked suspiciously. I didn't like the idea of ending up alone in a back alley with Mark and Jack. Not after what we'd done.

"On a date," he said bitterly. "As if nothing ever happened."

I didn't move.

"I won't hurt you, if that's what you're afraid of. I want to talk is all."

I watched his sullen, weary face a second before moving toward the door. The alley was dark and surprisingly silent as the door closed behind us. I stood motionless, waiting for my eyes to adjust and listening to make sure there were no extra footsteps. Pretty soon I could see Buster's big old Cadillac a few yards in front of me, but otherwise the alley seemed deserted.

174

"So what do you want with me?" My voice sounded weak and hollow, like when I have the flu or something.

"Sit down."

He climbed up on Buster's hood and sat with his back on the windshield. I did the same, hoping Buster wouldn't come out and catch us there. Neither of us said anything for a while, lying back, staring up past the rooftops at the stars. I buttoned my denim jacket against the cool breeze. It was really starting to feel like fall now and the air smelled clean and damp compared to the stuffy atmosphere of Buster's.

"You know what happened." It was more of a statement than a question.

"I know some. Other people do, too." I didn't want to be out there alone with Jack with him thinking I was the only one who knew anything.

"It was an accident. You know that, don't you?"

"People don't usually work so hard to cover up accidents."

"We were scared. It all happened so fast. Mark . . . we were both afraid of what his father would do if he found out about it. We took his keys . . . we even stole some of his beer, and got into the school without his permission."

"Mark doesn't seem too worried."

Jack stiffened.

"Sometimes I hate him. I don't sleep for a week, and he pretends like nothing happened, that the whole thing will just go away."

We were quiet a minute.

"You'll have to tell."

"I know. I guess I've known all week. I don't know

175

how I'll do it. My parents will . . . I don't know. I don't know what'll happen to me. To either of us."

Jack started to blubber, and I didn't know what to say. It was strange. A big guy like that crying next to me.

"You were trespassing. And it was an accident." I said it like it was no big deal, but I knew it was.

"It was more than an accident. We should have known better."

"How did it happen?"

Jack didn't say anything right away. He snuffed loudly.

"We were drinking. Drinking a lot, all three of us. Mark and I were doing flips off the diving board, and BooBoo wanted to try. We shouldn't have let him. He never was any good at things like that, even if he hadn't been drinking. But we . . ."

Jack leaned forward and buried his face in his hands, sobbing uncontrollably. I sat by feeling totally helpless.

"But we thought it was funny," he continued through the tears, "the way he was so clumsy jerking around in the air . . . and then belly-flopping. And he was like a little kid running back to the diving board, yelling for us to watch the next one."

"So what happened?"

"The last time he got on the diving board, still all excited, Mark and I sneaked into the locker room. We had all his clothes, and we hid behind the door with them. We wanted to scare him, you know, make him think we left him there all alone with no clothes."

Jack had stopped crying now, and his voice had become wooden and cold.

"We waited there, expecting him to come tearing through the door. But he never did. It was so quiet out here, we wondered what he was doing. After a while we went out to see what he was up to, and . . ."

He drew a deep breath and slumped back against the windshield.

"At first we didn't see anything and we laughed, thinking he was running around the school naked looking for us. Then we saw him. He was face down, lying there near the bottom of the pool."

"Didn't you try to save him?" I was sorry I said that.

"Of course we tried to save him!" Jack said angrily. "You think we wanted him to die? We dragged him out and tried to make him breathe . . . but it was too late. Way too late. I don't know . . . he must have hit his head on the board or something. He was dead."

"Didn't you want to call an ambulance?"

"I don't know. It's different when you're there. We were so scared I hardly remember what we did. Mark said we had to get him out of the school. Somehow we got him dressed, and Mark pulled the car up to the side door. I keep thinking about how we carried him out. It was awful. He was filled with water. It kept splashing out of his mouth."

Jack sat up and started sobbing again. I really felt sorry for him. I kept trying to picture myself in his place.

"And so you put him in the trunk and brought him to the quarry so everybody'd think he drowned on his own," I said, guessing the rest.

"Mark said it didn't matter what we did to him since he was dead anyway, and there was nothing anybody could do for him. Mark said we had to worry about ourselves now."

I put my hand on his shoulder.

"It must have been tough keeping that inside all week."

"It was a nightmare. It still is, and one that you don't wake up from." He rolled off the car and slammed his fist into Buster's fender. "And the thing that really gets me is how Mark goes on as if nothing happened, like it doesn't matter about BooBoo as long as we don't get caught. He made up that hitchhiker story so the police would have something to waste their time on."

"Maybe it bothers him," I said, jumping down beside him. "Maybe he just doesn't show it."

"I don't know. Remember how he was all excited when Beaver was going to beat up on you? BooBoo wasn't dead three days, and he couldn't wait to see some kid get smacked around. That doesn't sound like somebody who's too upset."

I remembered how happy Mark looked when he announced to Beaver that I was coming down the street. And he didn't even have anything against me then. Jack wasn't like Mark at all.

"Everybody messes up," I said, jumping in front of him. "But people will stand by you. You'd be surprised, really. And I ought to know. Messing up is a kind of hobby of mine."

"Thanks," he said, "but I'm not talking about hitting a baseball through a window or something. I wish I was."

"Neither am I. And I wish I was."

He laughed and then he stopped suddenly, like he all of a sudden remembered how bad things were.

"I suppose I might as well get this over with."

"Do you want me to go with you? I will."

"No, you're an all right kid, and I appreciate it. But this is something I have to take care of on my own." He tapped my arm and continued his grim march down the street. "I'll see you around."

"See you around."

I watched sadly as Jack shuffled toward the police station, his head down, hands jammed into his pockets.

"Good luck," I yelled.

That wasn't quite what I wanted to say, but what can you say to a guy at a time like that?

I turned back toward Buster's and stopped. I didn't want to go back in.

179

# XXII

T HE STREETLIGHT BUZZED overhead, vibrating through the air and charging it with a kind of restless energy. Things were quiet inside now. Through the big window across the street I could see the cop at the desk picking up the phone every once in a while, talking, then going back to his paper work. I couldn't tell if he was filling out official reports or doing a crossword puzzle or something like that. Jack had disappeared into the back room with a couple of cops quite a while ago. How long ago I couldn't tell. I had drifted off a few times into a fitful, delirious sleep with awful thoughts and scary pictures bouncing around my brain. I would wake with a jump and not remember right away where I was. And each time I woke up I was shaking more and freezing worse than the time before. By now I was nearly numb with cold.

What was I doing there? Did I blame myself for this? That'd be stupid. I didn't cause the accident. And Jack said himself he would have confessed sooner or later. So what was holding me to that bench on the edge of the lonely darkness of the park? Why couldn't I go home?

I won. So why wasn't I celebrating?

Car doors slammed and I sat up straight. Two state troopers marched briskly into the station, pausing briefly at the desk before disappearing into the room with Jack and the two village cops.

An old car pulled up behind the trooper car, and a man and a woman climbed out. I didn't recognize them.

"Don't tell me how to act!" the man snarled. "I think I know how to take care of my own son!"

"I'm only saying that you should listen, John. Listen to him before you fly off the handle."

She chased him up the sidewalk, tugging at his arm. He shook her hand off and plowed on ahead.

"I might have a few things to say myself. Did you ever think of that?"

Poor Jack.

The door closed behind them. The man waved his arms angrily at the desk cop, who hurried him into the back room with everybody else. The woman hung back for a few seconds, probably to apologize. The desk cop raised his hands and smiled.

I lay down on the bench and curled up, trying to save as much heat as I could. I was shaking something fierce. What was I waiting for? I didn't know. I couldn't think. I closed my eyes for the longest time. Sometimes I saw BooBoo floating up out of the dark water. Sometimes I saw Jack in a roomful of angry cops, and his mother was trying to keep his father from hitting him. Either way I'd wake suddenly with a sickening feeling in the pit of my stomach.

But I still stayed.

A hand was on my shoulder. A hand in my dream.

"Is this your new address?"

I opened my eyes and the hand stayed. But I had to have been dreaming the voice. That voice.

"You know, you do have a nice home, Tyler. When did you take up sleeping on park benches?"

I rolled my head back and saw my mother, looking like some golden-haired glowing angel under the street-light. I couldn't be awake. It didn't make sense.

I sat up, rubbed my eyes, and looked again, squinting. Mom was still there. She took off her long coat and wrapped it around me. Then she sat down and kissed my forehead, smoothing my hair back.

"Are you awake yet, honey?"

I stared at her, dazed. Then I touched her shoulder. She felt real enough, but it seemed like I was looking at her from some fuzzy dreamworld.

"I think so," I said, puzzled. "I don't know."

"Come on, Space Cadet," she said, gently shaking me. "Snap out of it."

Chris always called me Space Cadet when I woke up.

"What . . . What are you doing here?" I scrunched up inside her coat and stared at her. It still didn't make much sense.

"Oh, excuse me. Is this bench by invitation only?" She smiled. "I could ask you the same thing. Chuckie and I have been all over town looking for you."

"I'm sorry," I said weakly. That was the one thing I could always remember to say, no matter what.

"You know, I heard a rumor that there's a cute guy around here who's about to become a teenager. I was afraid there'd be a party and I'd miss it. Know anything about that?"

"I forgot. I . . . . I guess I've been busy."

"So I heard," Mom said, wrapping the coat collar

182

tighter around my neck. "Are you going to tell me why you're out here freezing on a park bench when you're supposed to be home in bed?"

"It's a long story."

"Chuckie told me most of it. You're some kind of kid, you know that?"

"I don't know. I guess I'm different if that's what you mean."

"Different in a good way," she said, and put her arm around me. "Tell me, honey, did something happen tonight?"

"Jack turned himself in. He told me the whole story, and he turned himself in over there." I pointed. "It looks pretty bad for him."

"He's inside now?"

I nodded, tears starting down my face. I couldn't stop them.

"Do you want to tell me about it?"

I nodded again and started telling her everything. I still couldn't stop crying. It was like after my father died, when I let myself go and cried for everything that ever went wrong in the world.

"It'll be all right," Mom said, wrapping her arms tighter around me and squeezing.

"You didn't see how scared he looked. And you didn't see his father."

"It'll be tough for him for a while, but believe me it'll be all right."

"Will he have to go to jail?"

"No, honey, he won't have to go to jail. It was an accident. Just a terrible accident."

"Mom," I said, sniffling and wiping away the last tears on my sleeve, "it was like . . . I don't know . . .

It was like a game or something. And I wanted to win . . . you know . . . to prove I was right. And I did . . . but . . ."

"But you found out that life isn't just good guys fighting bad guys?"

I looked at her. And suddenly I realized I'd been almost as dumb as those fans at that professional wrestling show, wanting to see people as either good guys or bad guys. And thinking how the good guys' job was to make sure the bad guys got everything they deserved. It'd been easier to think that, easier and less confusing . . . Only it wasn't that simple. Jack was no bad guy. And I knew Mark had his own problems. His whole family did.

"Everything's so complicated," I said. "Sometimes I don't know how to look at things."

"I know," Mom said. "And your problem is that you're smart enough and sensitive enough to realize that." She stood up. "Why don't we get you home now? There's nothing we can do here."

I stood up. My legs felt like rubber, but I was awake now, and just knowing Mom was there made things quite a bit better. I saw the desk cop looking our way, and I took the coat off.

"Leave it on, honey. You'll catch pneumonia."

"Come on, Mom. Be serious. It's a lady's coat. I'm not walking home in that."

"Oh, I get it," she said, nodding her head. "It's better to freeze to death than to be seen in your old mother's coat."

"I won't freeze," I said. "And your age has nothing to do with it. Please, don't make me wear it." I handed it to her like it was a stink bomb.

184

"All right," she said, "but let's hurry. Your hands are like ice."

As soon as we hit the sidewalk, a big black car pulled up and parked beside us. Mr. Blumberg got out first on the other side, and then Mark got out right next to us. He glared down at me. All I could think of was that I was glad I wasn't wearing Mom's coat.

"I hope you're happy now," Mark snarled, brushing past me.

"No," I said in a low voice, "I'm not."

Mr. Blumberg hesitated, looking over the car, first at me, then at my mother. He came around the side of the car.

"I'm sorry," he said. "I'm really sorry."

"That's all right," Mom said gently. "He's upset."

"No, what I mean is, I'm sorry about everything. Everything." He turned and hurried after his son.

Mom looked at me, puzzled. I knew nobody had told her what Mr. Blumberg had said about her.

"It's a long story," I said.

"Well, you can tell me later," she said, tugging my arm down the sidewalk. "I have a hunch your other birthday guest may have already arrived, and he'll be wondering where we are."

"Christopher? Is he coming home, too?" I stopped walking and looked at her.

"Could be. You never know." She smiled when she saw the look on my face.

"Wow," I said, thinking how great it would be to have everybody together again. "Excellent! Let's go."

Now I was towing Mom down the street.

"Oh, my God! It's after midnight," she said. "You

know what that means? My little baby is thirteen. I can't believe it. My little baby.''

I groaned.

''Oh, Mom, don't start in on that baby stuff. Especially not in front of Chris and Chuckie.''

''Then I'd better start getting it out of my system right now. I'd hate to embarrass you.''

She wrapped her arms around me, right on the street where everybody could see, and started squeezing me and planting kisses all over my face.

''Mom!'' I whined. ''Cut it out. Somebody'll see us.''

She laughed.

''I want everybody to see us. I want the whole world to know that my son is thirteen, and I love him more than ever!''

''Mom, please, don't make a . . .''

''I LOVE MY SON, EVERYBODY! I LOVE MY SON!''

''Oh, God, no Mom.'' I noticed some lights snapping on in the houses around us. ''Mom, come on. People . . .''

She pinched my cheeks.

''Pee-wul . . .''

''Oh, you are too cute. You really are. And I'm glad to see you're getting some color back in your cheeks.''

She laughed as I tried to cover my face. I hoped no one would recognize us. Talk about humiliation.

''Mom, I changed my mind. You can kiss me at home if you still need to.''

''Okay, but I'm first. Promise me that. I know for a fact Mrs. Saunders will try to crowd in ahead of me.''

I groaned again. Mom laughed and took off running.

"Come on, Tyler! You're getting slow."

Oh, great, I thought. She used my name. But I had to laugh, watching her tear down the street, whooping it up like a kid. After all, she was forty years old. I took off after her, feeling pretty good myself.

Who knows? Thirteen might turn out to be a good year for lemons.

## About the Author

DANIEL HAYES lives in Schaghiticoke (Skat-ti-kuk), New York, and teaches English at Troy High School. *The Trouble with Lemons* is his first novel.